FAME

FAME

A Novel in Nine Episodes

Daniel Kehlmann

Translated from the German by
Carol Brown Janeway

PANTHEON BOOKS, NEW YORK

Translation copyright © 2010 by Carol Brown Janeway

All rights reserved. Published in the United States by Pantheon Books, a division of Random House, Inc., New York, and in Canada by Random House of Canada Limited, Toronto. Originally published in Germany as *Ruhm: Ein Roman in neun Geschichten* by Rowohlt Verlag GmbH, Reinbek bei Hamburg, in 2009. Copyright © 2009 by Rowohlt Verlag GmbH, Reinbek bei Hamburg.

Pantheon Books and colophon are registered trademarks of Random House, Inc.

Library of Congress Cataloging-in-Publication Data

Kehlmann, Daniel, [date]
[Ruhm. English]
Fame : a novel in nine episodes / Daniel Kehlmann ; translated from the German by Carol Brown Janeway.
p.   cm.
ISBN 978-0-307-37871-2
I. Janeway, Carol Brown. II. Title.
PT2671.E32R8413 2010
833'.914—dc22   2009052380

www.pantheonbooks.com

Printed in the United States of America

First American Edition

2   4   6   8   9   7   5   3   1

For A and O

Contents

FAME

Voices

E ven before Ebling reached home, his cell phone rang. For years he had refused to buy one, because he was a technician and didn't trust the thing. Why did nobody wonder about whether it was a good idea to clutch a powerful source of radiation to your head? But Ebling had a wife, two children, and a handful of acquaintances, and one of them was always complaining that he was unreachable. So finally he'd given in and bought a phone, which he asked the guy he bought it from to activate immediately. In spite of himself, he was impressed: it was absolutely perfect, beautifully designed, smooth lines, elegant. And now, without warning, it was ringing.

Very hesitantly, he picked up.

A woman asked for someone called Raff, Ralf, or Rauff, he couldn't figure out the name. A mistake, he said, wrong number. She apologized and hung up.

That evening, the next call. "Ralf!" The man's voice was

loud and hoarse. "What gives, what are you up to, you old bastard?"

"Wrong number!" Ebling sat up in bed. It was already past ten o'clock and his wife was looking at him reproachfully.

The man apologized, and Ebling switched off the phone.

Next morning there were three messages. He listened to them in the subway on the way to work. A giggling woman asked him to call her back. A man yelled that he should come over right away, they weren't going to wait for him much longer; you could hear music and the clink of glasses in the background. And then the same woman again: "Ralf, come on, where are you?"

Ebling sighed and called Customer Service.

Strange, said the representative, sounding bored. Simply couldn't happen. Nobody was given a number already assigned to somebody else. There were all sorts of security measures to prevent it.

"But that's what's happened."

No, said the woman. Absolutely impossible.

"And what are you going to do about it?"

She said she had no idea. Because the whole thing was impossible.

Ebling opened his mouth, then shut it again. He knew that someone else in his shoes would have lost it—but that wasn't his sort of thing, he was no good at it. He hit the off button.

Seconds later, it rang again. "Ralf?" said a man.

"No."

"What?"

"This number is . . . There's been a mistake—you've misdialed."

"This is Ralf's number!"

Ebling hung up and stuck the phone in the pocket of his jacket. The subway was jammed again, so he was having to stand today as well. On one side a man with a big moustache was glaring at him as if he were his sworn enemy. There were a lot of things about his life that Ebling didn't like. It bothered him that his wife's mind was always somewhere else, that she read such stupid books, and that she was such a lousy cook. It bothered him that he didn't have a smart son, and that he didn't understand his daughter at all. It bothered him that he could always hear his neighbors snoring through the party walls, which were way too thin. But what bothered him most of all was being on the subway at rush hour. Always packed in, always jammed full, and always the same stink.

But he liked his work. He and dozens of his coworkers sat under very bright lamps examining defective computers sent in by dealers from all over the country. He knew how fragile the brains of the little disks were, how complex and mysterious. No one fully understood how they functioned; no one could say for sure why they suddenly broke down or went haywire. For a long time now nobody had attempted to establish the root causes, they simply substituted one component or another until the whole thing started working again. He often thought about just how much in the world depended on these machines, bearing in mind what an exception, even a miracle, it was if they actually did the things they were supposed to. In the evenings, half asleep, he was so troubled by this idea—all the airplanes, all the electronically guided weaponry, the entire banking system—that his heart began to race. That's when Elke snapped at him, saying why couldn't he just lie there quietly, she might as well be sharing her bed with a cement mixer, and he would apologize, thinking that his mother had long since been the one to tell him that he was too sensitive.

As he was getting out of the subway car, the phone rang. It was Elke, telling him to buy cucumbers on the way home tonight: the supermarket in their street was offering a special on them.

Ebling said he would and hung up fast. It rang again and a woman asked him if he'd thought it over, only an idiot would give up someone like her. Or did he see it differently?

No, he said without thinking, that's how he saw it too.

"Ralf!" She laughed.

Ebling's heart thumped, and his throat was dry. He hung up.

He was confused and nervous the whole way to the office. Obviously an original owner of this number had a voice similar to his own. He called Customer Service again.

No, said a woman, they couldn't just give him another number unless he paid for it.

"But this number already belongs to someone else!"

Impossible, she said. There were—

"Security measures, I know! But I keep getting calls for . . . You know, I'm a technician myself. I know you're inundated with calls from people who are absolutely clueless. But this is my area. I know how—"

Nothing she could do, she said. She would pass on his request.

"And then? What happens next?"

Then, she said, they'd see. But that wasn't part of her job.

That morning he couldn't concentrate on his work. His hands trembled and he had no appetite during his lunch break, even though there was Wiener schnitzel on the menu. The canteen didn't have it very often, and normally he was already looking forward to it the day before. But this time he put his tray back on the rack with his plate still half full, went off to a quiet corner of the dining room, and switched on his phone.

Three messages. His daughter, wanting to be picked up from her ballet class. This was a surprise to him because he hadn't even known she was taking dancing. A man, saying please call back. There was nothing in his message to suggest which one of them he meant: Ebling or the other one. And then a woman, wanting to know why he was making himself scarce. This voice, deep and caressing, was one he hadn't heard before. Just as he was about to disconnect, the phone rang again. The number on the screen began with a plus sign and 22. Ebling didn't know which country code that was. He knew almost nobody in other countries, just his cousin in Sweden and a huge old woman in Minneapolis who sent a photograph of herself every year at Christmas, raising a glass with a big grin. *To all the dear Eblings* it said on the back, and neither he nor Elke had a clue which one of them she was related to. He picked up.

"Are we seeing each other next month?" a man asked loudly. "You're going to the Lucerne festival, aren't you? They're not going to make it without you, not the way things are, Ralf, you know?"

"I'll be there," said Ebling.

"That guy Lohmann. Should have expected it. Have you spoken to Degetel's people?"

"Not yet."

"C'mon, it's time! Lucerne can really help, like Venice three years ago." The man laughed. "Apart from that? Clara?"

"Yes, yes," said Ebling.

"You old dog," said the man. "Unbelievable."

"I think so too," said Ebling.

"D'you have a cold? You sound funny."

"I have to . . . go do something. I'll call you back."

"Okay. You never change, do you?"

The man hung up. Ebling leaned against the wall and rubbed his forehead. He needed a moment to get ahold of himself: this was the canteen, he was surrounded by coworkers eating schnitzel. At that moment Rogler was going past, carrying his tray.

"Hello, Ebling," said Rogler. "Everything okay?"

"Sure." Ebling switched off the phone.

The whole afternoon, he couldn't focus. The question of which part in a particular computer was defective, and how anyone could have arrived at the errors described in the dealers' cryptic reports—*customer says re-set activ. imm. bef. display but indic. zero* — just didn't interest him today. It was the same feeling you got when something was making you happy.

He prolonged the moment. The phone stayed silent during the subway ride home, it stayed silent while he shopped for cucumbers in the supermarket, and all during dinner with Elke and the two children, who kept kicking each other under the table, it slumbered in his pocket, but he couldn't stop thinking about it.

Then he went down to the cellar. It smelled of mildew, there was a pile of beer crates in one corner, and the component parts of a temporarily disassembled IKEA wardrobe in another. Ebling switched on the phone. Two messages. Just as he was going to listen to them, the gadget vibrated in his hand: someone was calling.

"Yes?"

"Ralf?"

"Yes?"

"Now what?" She laughed. "Are you playing games with me?"

"I'd never do that."

"Pity!"

His hand shook. "You're right. In fact, I'd . . . like to . . ."

"Yes?"

". . . play with you."

"When?"

Ebling looked around. He knew this cellar better than any place in the world. He had put every object in it there himself. "Tomorrow. You say when and where. I'll be there."

"You mean it?"

"Up to you to find out."

He heard her take a deep breath. "*Pantagruel.* Nine o'clock. You make the reservation."

"Will do."

"You know this is crazy?"

"Who's to care?"

She laughed and hung up.

That night he reached for his wife for the first time in a very long time. At first she was simply incredulous, then she asked what had come over him and had he been drinking, then she gave in. It was quick, and even as he felt her still underneath him, it seemed to him that they were doing something transgressive. A hand tapped his shoulder: she couldn't breathe! He apologized, but it was another few minutes before he pulled away and rolled over on his side. Elke switched on the light, gave him a disapproving look, and retreated to the bathroom.

Of course he didn't go to Pantagruel. He left the phone switched off all day, and at nine o'clock he was sitting in front of the TV with his son watching a second division soccer match. He felt an electrical prickling, it was as if he had a doppelgänger, his representative in a parallel universe, who was entering an expensive restaurant at this very moment to meet a tall, beautiful woman who hung on his words, who laughed when he said something witty, and who brushed her hand against his, now and again, as if by accident.

At half time he went down to the cellar and switched on the phone. No message. He waited. No one called. After half an hour he switched it off again and went to bed; he couldn't go on pretending that soccer interested him.

He couldn't get to sleep, and shortly after midnight he got up and groped his way back into the cellar, barefoot and in his nightshirt. He switched on the phone. Four messages. Before he could listen to them, the phone rang.

"Ralf," said a man. "Sorry I'm calling so late . . . but it's important! Malzacher is insisting that the two of you meet tomorrow. The whole project may be on the skids. Morgenheim will be there too. You know what's at stake!"

"I don't care," said Ebling.

"Are you nuts?"

"We'll see."

"You really are nuts!"

"Morgenheim's bluffing," said Ebling.

"You've certainly got balls."

"Yes," said Ebling. "I do."

When he wanted to listen to his messages, his phone rang again.

"You shouldn't have done that!" Her voice was hoarse and forced.

"If you knew," said Ebling. "I had a terrible day."

"Don't lie."

"Why should I lie?"

"It's all because of her, isn't it? Are you two . . . together . . . again?"

Ebling said nothing.

"At least you could admit it!"

"Don't talk nonsense!" He wondered which of the women whose voices he knew was the one she meant. He would like to have known more about Ralf's life; after all, it was now, to a small extent, his life too. What did Ralf actually do, how did he make a living? Why did some people get everything and other people almost nothing? Some people achieved so much and other people didn't, merit had nothing to do with it.

"I'm sorry," she said softly. "It's often . . . hard with you."

"I know."

"But someone like you—you're not like everyone else."

"I'd love to be like everyone else," said Ebling. "But I've never understood how to do it."

"So, tomorrow?"

"Tomorrow," said Ebling.

"If you don't show up again, we're over."

As he crept soundlessly back upstairs, he wondered whether Ralf actually existed. Suddenly he found it unbelievable that Ralf was living out there, going about his business, oblivious to him, Ebling. Perhaps Ralf's life had always been intended for him, and some mere accident had switched their destinies.

The phone rang again. He picked up, listened to a couple of sentences, and cried, "Cancel it!"

"Excuse me?" asked a woman, her voice shocked. "He came specially, we've worked so hard for this meeting, so that . . ."

"I'm not dependent on him." Who could this be about? He would have given a lot to know.

"Of course you are!"

"We'll see." A rush of euphoria such as he had never felt before surged through him.

"If you say so."

"I certainly do!"

Ebling had to fight the temptation to find out what all this was actually about. He had worked out that he could say anything provided he didn't ask any questions, but that people got suspicious the moment he wanted to know something. Yesterday a woman whose throaty voice he particularly liked had accused him directly of not being Ralf—all because he'd asked where in Andalusia they'd been together on summer vacation three years ago. That way he'd never learn more about this man. Once he'd stopped in front of a poster for the new Ralf Tanner movie, imagining for a few dizzying seconds that maybe he had the legendary actor's phone number, and it was his friends, his colleagues, and his mistresses he'd been talking to for the past week. It was just possible: Tanner's voice and his own were quite similar. But then he'd shaken his head with a lopsided smile and gone on his way. In any case, it couldn't go on much longer. He had no illusions, sooner or later the mistake would be corrected and his phone would go silent.

"Ah, you again. I couldn't come to Pantagruel. She's back."

"Katja? You mean—you're back with Katja?"

Ebling nodded and scribbled the name on a scrap of paper. He thought the woman he was talking to was named Carla, but he didn't yet have enough clues to risk calling her that. It was unfortunate that nobody announced themselves on the phone anymore: the numbers came up on the screen and everyone went on the assumption that the other party already knew who the caller was before they picked up.

"I won't forgive you."

"I'm so sorry."

"Bullshit. You're not sorry!"

"I swear." Ebling smiled as he leaned against the side of the wardrobe. "Or maybe not. Katja's amazing."

She yelled for awhile. She cursed him and made threats and then even ended up crying. But because it was Ralf, finally, who had unleashed this chaos, Ebling didn't have to feel guilty. Heart thumping, he listened to her. He had never been so close to the very heart of an exciting woman.

"Pull yourself together!" he cut in. "There was no way it was going to work, you know that!"

After she'd hung up, he stood there for a time, feeling a little faint, listening to the silence, as if Carla's sobs were still echoing somewhere.

When he encountered Elke in the kitchen, he was so astonished he felt rooted to the spot. For a moment, he'd believed she came from another life, or a dream that had no connection with reality. That night he pulled her close again, and this time too she gave in to him reluctantly, and all the while he imagined Carla, swept away by passion.

Next day he was alone at home, and called one of the numbers for the first time. "It's me. Just checking everything's okay."

"What's this?" a man's voice asked.

"Ralf!"

"Which Ralf?"

Ebling hastily hit the disconnect button, then tried again with another of the numbers.

"Ralf, my God! I tried you yesterday . . . I . . . I . . ."

"Easy!" said Ebling, disappointed that again it wasn't a woman. "What's up?"

"I can't go on like this."

"Then stop."

"There's no way out."

"There's always a way out." Ebling couldn't stop yawning.

"Ralf, are you telling me I . . . finally have to take the consequences? That I have to go all the way?"

Ebling went channel-surfing. But he was out of luck, there seemed to be nothing around but folk music and carpenters doing things with planks, and repeats of old series from the eighties: the whole afternoon-TV gloom. How was he even seeing all this, why was he at home and not at work? He had no idea. Was it possible he'd simply forgotten to go in?

"I'm going to swallow the whole container."

"Go right ahead." Ebling reached for the book that was lying on the table. *The Way of the Self to the Self,* by Miguel Auristos Blanco. The sun's disk on the jacket. It was Elke's. He pushed it away with the tips of his fingers.

"Everything comes to you just like that, Ralf. You get it all on a platter. You have no idea what it's like always coming second. Being one in a crowd, always someone's last choice. You have no idea!"

"That's true."

"I'm going to do it—I mean it!"

Ebling switched off, just in case this pathetic person tried to call him back.

That night he dreamed about hares. They were large, there was nothing cute about them, they emerged from dense thickets, they looked more like filthy beasts than the charming little creatures from animated films, and they stared at him with eyes that glowed red. Behind him there was a cracking sound in the bushes, he swung round, but his movement shook everything loose, reality melted away, and he heard Elke saying it was unendurable, how could anyone breathe that loudly, enough was enough and she wanted her own bedroom.

Starting the next morning, the phone was silent. He waited and listened, but it didn't ring. When it finally did so in the early afternoon, it was his boss wanting to know why he hadn't come in the last two days, if he was feeling ill, and if his doctor's certificate had somehow got mislaid. Ebling apologized and coughed for good measure, and when his boss said it wasn't serious, these things happened, no reason to get excited, he was a good worker and everyone knew his worth, he felt tears of rage in his eyes.

The next day he sabotaged three computers and installed a hard drive in such a way that all the data on it would erase themselves exactly one month later. His telephone was silent.

He came close a few times to calling one of the numbers. His thumb was on the call-back button and he imagined that only a second separated him from hearing one of the voices. If he'd had more courage, he'd have pressed it. Or started a fire somewhere. Or gone in search of Carla.

At least there was Wiener schnitzel for lunch. Twice in one week—a rare treat. Rogler sat opposite him, chewing religiously. "The new E14," he said with his mouth full. "It's enough to drive you crazy. There isn't a damn thing inside it that works. Anyone who buys it has only himself to blame."

Ebling nodded.

"But what are we supposed to do?" Rogler was getting loud. "It's new. I want it too! There's nothing else on the market."

"True," said Ebling. "There's nothing else."

"Hey," said Rogler. "Stop staring at your phone."

Ebling twitched and put it in his pocket.

"Not so long ago you didn't want anything to do with one, and now you don't budge an inch without it. Just relax—nothing can be that urgent." Rogler hesitated for a moment. He swallowed, then stuck another piece of schnitzel in his mouth. "Please don't take this the wrong way. But who would be calling you anyhow?"

In Danger

A novel without a protagonist! Do you get it? A structure, the connections, a narrative arc, but no main character, no hero advancing throughout."

"Interesting," said Elisabeth wearily.

He looked at his watch. "Why are we running late again? It was the same thing yesterday, what are they doing, why does it keep happening?"

"Because stuff happens."

"Did you notice the man over there, he looks like a dog on its hind legs! But what causes those delays, why can't they experiment just once, just like that, and try taking off *on time*?"

She sighed. There were more than two hundred people in the departure lounge. Many of them were asleep, a few others were reading crudely printed newspapers. The portrait of some bearded politician grinned down off the wall under a gaudy flag. A kiosk offered magazines, detective novels, spir-

itual self-help books by Miguel Auristos Blanco, and ciga-
rettes.

"Do you think these airplanes are safe? I mean, they're
really ancient equipment sold on by the Europeans. With us,
they'd never even be allowed to take off, it's no secret, right?"

"No."

"Excuse me?"

"It's no secret."

Leo massaged his forehead, cleared his throat, opened and
shut his mouth, and blew his nose at considerable length,
then looked at her with watering eyes. "Was that a joke?"

She didn't reply.

"They should have told me up front, they shouldn't have
invited me, I mean, where are the rules? They can't invite me
if it's unsafe! Did you see the woman over there, she's writing
something down. Why? What's she writing? Say, you were
joking, weren't you, about these planes—they're not really
dangerous?"

"No, no," she said, "don't worry."

"You're just saying that to make me feel better!"

She closed her eyes.

"I knew it. I can tell. See over there! If we were in a story,
we'd be part of this group, and they'd forget us before we
even took off. Who knows how that could develop!"

"Why should anything develop? We'd catch the next
plane."

"If there is one!"

Elisabeth said nothing. She wished she could sleep, it was

still early, but she knew he would never allow it until after they'd landed. She would have to spend the entire flight explaining to him that flying was perfectly safe and there was no need to worry about a crash. After that she'd have to take care of the luggage and in the hotel it would be her job to speak to the receptionist and arrange for room service to send something up that Leo would agree to eat, given his juvenile tastes in food. And in the late afternoon she'd have to make sure that Leo was ready when they came to collect him for his lecture.

"I think things are starting to move!" he cried.

At the other end of the departure lounge a young woman had taken up a position at one of the counters. People began to stand up, gather their belongings, and shuffle in that direction.

"It's still going to be some time," said Elisabeth.

"We'll miss the flight!"

"They've only just started. They'll be another half hour at least."

"They're going to leave without us!"

"Please, why would they—"

But he was already on his feet and in the line. She crossed her arms and watched his skinny figure inch its way forward. Finally it was his turn, he showed his boarding card, and disappeared into the walkway to the plane. She waited. Fifteen, twenty, thirty minutes passed, and people were still boarding. When there was nobody left, she got up and boarded within seconds. Pushing her way down the center aisle, she sat down next to Leo.

"You have no right to do that! I thought you weren't coming. I was already working out how to stop them taking off, but I can't make myself understood here, I can't explain things to anyone."

She apologized.

"No, really, it's all exhausting enough as it is, I can't cope with more . . . Did you see the two children up front, they're weird. Particularly the little girl. Green eyes! They're flying on their own, without their parents."

"Impressive," she said.

He took a long look at her. "I'm pathetic," he said finally. "Aren't I?"

"Well, yes."

"I'm insufferable."

She bobbed her head.

"I'd understand if you wanted to go home. Of course if you did, I'd fly home too. I couldn't get through it without you. The whole thing was a mistake anyway, I should never have agreed, absolutely idiotic. Shall we just go home? Right now?"

"Please. Give it fifteen minutes. Please, just settle down."

He fell silent. And he actually managed to get a grip on himself and keep quiet for the next ten minutes while the plane accelerated, took off, and soared into the sky.

They had met six weeks earlier at a particularly boring party, and it was only after she'd been talking to him for some time that it dawned on Elisabeth that the strange but intelligent man who kept cracking his knuckles and staring at the ceiling was none other than Leo Richter, the author of intricate short stories full of complicated mirror effects and unpredictable shifts and swerves that were flourishes of empty virtuosity. She had recently read his collection about the doctor Lara Gaspard, and naturally she knew his most famous story, the one about the old woman on her way to an assisted-suicide clinic in Switzerland. They had met again the next day, already that evening she went with him to his sparsely furnished apartment, and to her surprise, Leo in bed demonstrated a decisiveness for which she was totally unprepared. She had dug her fingernails into his back, rolled her eyes up under their lids, and bitten his shoulder, and as she was on her way home in the dawn after several hours that left her totally spent, she knew that she wanted to see him again and that perhaps there was room for him in her life.

She soon discovered all the aspects of his personality: his anxiety attacks and neuroses, the sudden waves of euphoria that came out of nowhere, and the periods of total concentration during which he seemed to vanish inside himself and if she so much as spoke to him, he looked at her as if he had no idea what she was doing there.

For his part, he was fascinated by her job. By her activities with Doctors Without Borders—had she really done parachute jumps, with a real parachute? In a real war zone?

At this point, she always changed the subject. She knew that curiosity was part and parcel of his makeup and his métier, but there were things she didn't wish to talk about. Anyone who hadn't lived through such things personally would be likely to take it all as mere phrasemaking and anecdotage; words failed to capture the reality. What it felt like to amputate a man's legs under inadequate anesthetic, to drag him across fields in the shimmering heat, only to lose him a few feet from the waiting helicopter, so that the entire effort was pointless, and then on the flight back to realize that entire portions of the previous days had erased themselves from your memory, that there were blank spaces, as if you'd had experiences that were so extreme and alien that they had no firm foothold in reality and were unavailable to the mind. How should she have described these things? As an old doctor had said to her years ago, people who have experienced nothing love to tell stories while people who have experienced a great deal suddenly have no stories to tell at all. But she knew that Leo intuited certain things. She had the same profession as his heroine Lara Gaspard, they were the same age, and if she was right about his sparse descriptions of Lara's appearance, the two of them also looked rather alike. This must be another reason why he found her interesting. She often noticed that he watched her with an almost scientific focus, his lips moving as if he were taking mental notes.

A few weeks previously, he had given a lecture at the Academy of Mainz about the ongoing death of culture and the fact that this was not necessarily a bad thing, since humanity would be in better shape without the burden of knowledge and tradition. This was now the age of the image, of the sounds of rhythms and a mystical dissolution into the eternal present—a religious ideal become reality through the power of technology. Nobody could figure out whether he was being serious or ironic, whether he was a nihilist or a conservative, but this was precisely the reason why the text was reprinted, all sorts of responses were solicited, and German cultural institutes all around the world invited him on lecturing tours. On a whim, he had agreed to do a circuit through Central America, and when he'd asked Elisabeth if she'd like to come along, to her own surprise she hadn't even thought twice.

Shortly before they landed, Leo fell into a restless sleep. Elisabeth was dreading what would come next: at their last stop, the moment they were in the airport he had been literally paralyzed with disgust at the sight of the head of the cultural institute in her traditional woolen jacket. He had sat in the car with Elisabeth in silence, jaw clenched, and had even reached for her hand when they were stopped at a police checkpoint. Nothing happened, of course, and the agents had immediately waved them on, but when they reached the hotel, he was totally undone, covered in sweat and terrified. He spent the entire afternoon locked in their double room before giving his evening lecture to twenty-seven Germans in a badly lit hall, after which the lady director of the cultural institute had insisted on taking them to the only pizzeria in town, where she had plied Leo with questions about where he got his ideas from and did he write in the mornings or the afternoons. He then spent half the night in lamentation, pacing up and down the room and cursing his fate until finally, more out of desperation than passion, the two of them fell onto the bed in each other's arms. At five in the morning her cell phone rang, and she was told that three of her closest coworkers had just been abducted in Africa.

"Did you see?" Leo was awake again, tapping her shoulder and pointing to the outside beyond the portholes. "Like a great big stage set. A grid with hundreds of lightbulbs. Maybe we're not flying at all, maybe we're not even here. Maybe it's all a trick. And besides, what do we do if there's no one there to pick us up? I've got a feeling, and I'm not often wrong. You watch."

The lady from the cultural institute who was waiting was named Rappenzilch, wore a traditional woolen jacket, and had buckteeth. Her first question to Leo was where he got his ideas from. Elisabeth listened to her voicemail. She felt hollowed out by fear.

They were sitting in the car. Outside the little cubes that were the houses in the capital streamed by in the pale morning light. Shop signs, under them old women walking with their baskets of fruit, in the sky the yellowish smoke from distant factories.

In the hotel, she called headquarters in Geneva. Her colleague Moritz, still at his desk though it was long past midnight, told her the situation was confused, the UN couldn't help, and they had to assume the regime was complicit. Two years ago, when she was in that country, hadn't she had personal dealings with a secretary of state?

"Yes." Her voice echoed off the tiled walls in the bathroom. "One of the worst."

"Worst or not, the way things are right now, you're the only connection we've got."

She went back into the bedroom where Leo was sitting on the bed looking at her reproachfully. This Mrs. Rappenzilch! And her teeth! And back on another damn podium tonight, he'd absolutely had it! He turned on the TV. Pictures of soldiers marching, then the faces of some politicians, then more soldiers. Leo shook his head and started ranting about the metaphysical horror this spectacle induced in him: the feeling of being a prisoner, this whole part of the world was its own unique hell, you just knew instinctively you'd never get out. You'd have to be nuts to put yourself willingly in a situation like this. "Look, they're not even marching in step. They can't even manage that! Did you see her teeth?!"

"Whose teeth?"

"Mrs. Rappenzilch's!"

She went back into the bathroom to make more calls. Leo mustn't notice, it all had to remain secret, who knew what he might blurt out. She called an underling of the African secretary of state whom she'd gotten to know some years before in unpleasant circumstances. She had to try six times before she got through, the ringtone sounded strange and the sound quality was dreadful. The man said he'd see what he could do. She thanked him effusively, hung up, and had to fight the urge to crumple up onto the floor. Her stomach hurt, and there was a pounding ache in her head.

When she came back into the room, Leo was on the hotel phone bawling somebody out. "It's unacceptable, I refuse to be treated like this! No!" He threw down the receiver, turned to her, and said triumphantly: "Roebrich."

She had no idea who Roebrich was, but the way he'd said the name suggested that this must be some important person in literary circles.

"The prize. They more or less promised it to me and now suddenly they want to take it back, all because I don't want Eldrich giving the presentation speech. Unacceptable! Maybe they can do that with Reuke or Moehrsam, but not with— just look at the sky! The sun playing on those clouds of gas, it makes them look beautiful, not like filthy pollution. Everything looks beautiful if you see it against the sun. Anyhow, I told him he can forget it. If he wants me on the jury next year, then we're going to play by my rules!"

She sank down onto the bed. She'd been with Carl, Henri, and Paul in Somalia the year before. On the last day, Carl had told her that he wouldn't be doing this much longer, his nerves wouldn't take it anymore, and it wasn't good for the soul either. What were they doing to the three of them right now, in what unlit room, inaccessible to every rational force on the planet? She lay there motionless, and all of a sudden, out of nowhere, she was engaged in a conversation with four policemen who'd morphed into one and the same person, she had no idea how, whom she had to answer correctly, no mistakes allowed, though the questions were all about her childhood and involved the most complex calculations, because every wrong answer meant that someone would die. A hand came down on her shoulder and she woke up with a scream.

"I knew you had nightmares at night—that's why they're called nightmares. But nightmares in the afternoon—that's new. You were whimpering like a child."

She said she couldn't remember a thing. He looked at her appraisingly and to evade his glance she went into the bathroom to take a shower. Letting the hot water run over her head, she tried not to think about Carl, Henri, and Paul. After all, they were grown men who were fully aware of the risks they took, men who knew how to handle life, and who were made of different . . . in short, they were men who could take care of themselves.

Mrs. Rappenzilch came to collect them. During the journey to the cultural institute she regaled them with stories of attacks and muggings. This was a very dangerous city. An agitated Leo pulled out his notebook.

At the institute they were awaited by thirty-two Germans. Leo went to the podium and, as always, immediately shed all sense of oppression and fatigue. He stood up straight and made acute observations about culture and barbarism, noise, blood, and danger—Elisabeth noticed that he was deviating from his written text, the last few days had inspired him. Even when he was improvising, his sentences were perfectly formed, and he radiated a concentrated energy that made it impossible to look away. Then her phone rang and she had to hurry out into the corridor.

His Excellency, said the secretary of state's underling, was not opposed to a conversation, and she would receive further word tomorrow. She uttered her groveling thanks and called

Moritz. He told her the Foreign Ministry had weighed in, but one should hope for nothing from the politicians, and the German Secret Service presence in the region was insignificant. They were going to have to rely on themselves.

When she came back, Leo had just finished and people were applauding. Then he signed about a dozen books and answered three questions about where he got his ideas from. Soon Mrs. Rappenzilch, suddenly in a nervous state and bright red in the face, was urging him to finish: the consul general was waiting, the reception had already begun!

"Why do they always ask that?" Leo whispered in the car. "Where do I get my ideas from. What kind of a question is that, what am I supposed to say?"

"Well, what do you tell them?"

"Bathtub."

"Excuse me?"

"I say I get all my ideas in the bathtub. That does it for them. They're happy. Look, over there, a Ralf Tanner poster! He really is everywhere, you can't get away from him even on the other side of the world. I met him last year. What a clown! But what's that over there?" He leaned forward and tapped Mrs. Rappenzilch on the shoulder. "What's going on there, do you see, has someone been attacked?"

Mrs. Rappenzilch turned her head but they'd already passed the scene and the mob was no longer visible. Perfectly possible, she said, it was a common occurrence.

Leo wrote something in his notebook.

The official residence was on a hill high above the flickering lights of the city. The sky was black and the cloud cover low, no stars to be seen. Liveried men carried little trays around, and everywhere there were Germans standing, shoulders back, serious expressions, glass in hand, stiff, looking grimly earnest.

Five men immediately surrounded Leo; she could see him trying to catch her eye. His look was murderous. He seemed to be radiating waves of sheer destructiveness of such force that everyone there would have to sense them. "In the bathtub," he was saying. "All my ideas. Always."

A thin man blocked her path, held out his hand, and said, "Charmed, von Stueckenbrock." It took her a moment to realize he was introducing himself. A second man joined them and said, "Delighted, Becker!" Then a third: "Seifert. Siemens. I run Siemens. Local operations, that is." Then he launched into a long account of how he'd read Leo's most recent book on the train from Bebra to Dortmund. Interesting, wasn't it?

"Indeed," she said, searching his face for some trace of irony, humor, anything.

Stueckenbrock asked where her husband got his ideas from.

"Who? Oh, I see, no, he's not my—in the bathtub."

"Oh," said Becker.

All three men leaned forward.

"His ideas," she said, "that's where he always has them. In the bathtub."

"Remarkable," said Seifert.

"Your first time here?" asked Becker.

She nodded.

The conversation died. The three men stood around her in silence: rigid, knotted up inside, prisoners of themselves, cast up by fate on the shores of a hideous place far distant from their equally hideous homeland. Elisabeth opened her mouth and shut it again, unable to think of a thing to say. She felt as if she was being made to talk to washing machines, or fire hydrants, or robots with whom she had no common language. Then her phone rang. For the first time in days it was a relief. Excusing herself with an apologetic gesture, she ran out.

It was only a journalist who'd dug up her number and wanted to know if the abduction story was true.

No comment, she said, but if he would wait until tomorrow, there might be a story.

He asked in a hostile way if that was all. Was there nothing else she could give him?

"Not right now," she said, "sorry."

Back in their hotel room, Leo immediately began to complain. These people! Did they have to be so *stupid*?

"Their lives aren't easy," she said. "None of them has had the career they hoped for. None of them is living where they wanted. Do you think they actually want to be here?"

She looked out of the window. Ralf Tanner's face was staring at her from the poster on the building opposite, so gigantically enlarged that it was no longer human. She found herself thinking about the scandal she'd just read about somewhere: Tanner had been set upon in a hotel lobby by a woman who screamed at him and slapped his face. Several tourists had filmed it and now it was on YouTube. And if Carl, Henri, and Paul were shot, beheaded, stoned, or burned alive, there was a good chance people would be able to see that too.

"I can't go on!" said Leo. "Do you know how often I've been asked today where I get my ideas from? Fourteen. And nine times whether I work in the morning or the afternoon. And eight times people have told me what trip they were on when they read something of mine. And the food was disgusting. Next month I'm supposed to be in Central Asia. I just can't. I'm going to cancel."

"Where are you meant to go?"

"Turkmenistan, I think. Or Uzbekistan. Who can tell the difference? Some writers' junket."

"Why ever did you accept?" she asked, incredulous.

He shrugged. "You're supposed to see the world. Confront things. You're not supposed to avoid all dangers."

"Dangers?"

He nodded.

Of course her reaction was too extreme, and once it had passed, she had to ask herself what had come over her, since they had never had a fight before. But just at that moment she could no longer control herself. What did he think he was talking about? He'd never once been in danger in his entire life, he needed help even to tie his own shoes, he was afraid of spiders and airplanes and went to pieces if a train was late! Driving through cities in cars under the protection of bureaucrats wasn't dangerous, it was a joke, and she couldn't take his whining for one more minute.

He didn't say a word, but watched her attentively, almost with curiosity, arms crossed. She didn't stop until she lost her voice. Her fury had exhausted itself. She looked around for her suitcase. Time to leave. It was over.

"Exactly!" he said.

"Excuse me?"

"This is how it could go. Two people traveling together. She has real responsibilities; he is always sniveling, and a pain in the ass. Lara Gaspard and her new lover. A painter. But . . ." He fell silent for a moment and seemed to be listening to some inner voice. "But she knows he's a genius. In spite of everything." He sat down at the little hotel writing desk and began to scribble.

She waited, but he'd obviously forgotten she was there. She lay down in bed, pulled the covers over her head, and was asleep in a matter of minutes.

When she woke up, he was still there—either he hadn't moved, or he was back there—at the desk. Pale predawn light was filtering through the window. She vaguely remembered that they'd made love during the night. He had come to bed and turned her onto her back, and in the half dark under the bedclothes they'd come together in exhaustion and a strange state of rage. Or had she dreamed it? Her memory wasn't too reliable, probably posttraumatic stress disorder, but it wasn't something she could talk to him about, because he would only use it somehow.

It wasn't until she reached the airport that she called Geneva. Apparently, said Moritz, the three of them were alive. The Foreign Ministry had nobody reliable on the spot, he didn't know of anyone who could be trusted with the negotiations. "The secretary of state?"

"If all goes well, I'll be speaking to him today."

"Where are you, actually?"

"Don't ask. Long story." She let the hand holding the phone drop, Leo was already lining up at the departure gate, although none of the boarding personnel had yet appeared. She signaled to him, he shook his head violently, and waved to her to hurry up and join him. "I'll call you back later."

In arrivals, they were met by a Mrs. Riedergott from the cultural institute. She was wearing a woolen jacket and thick spectacles. Her hair was pinned up, and her face seemed to be made of congealed pastry. "Mr. Richter, where do you get all your ideas?"

"Bathtub," said Leo, eyes closed.

"And tell me, do you write . . ."

"Always in the afternoons."

She thanked him for the information. The humidity made damp clouds in the streets, a president's face grinned down off the wall posters, and whenever the traffic lights turned red, half-naked children jumped into the road and performed tricks.

"I'm very tired," said Leo. "As soon as my lecture is over this evening I need to leave."

"Out of the question," said Mrs. Riedergott. "The ambassador's expecting you. A big reception, it's all been planned for weeks."

At the hotel Leo called the PEN Club and canceled the trip to Central Asia. Please would they turn to someone else, Maria Rubinstein the crime writer for example, she'd been saying to him only recently that she'd like to start doing more. He then sent a text message to Maria: *Possible trip, v. interesting, alas can't, PLS accept, I owe you, PLS thanksthanksthanks L.* Then he spent some time complaining to Elisabeth about Mrs. Riedergott: her face, her total impassivity, her stolid arrogance. Was there anything worse than these people?

"Yes," said Elisabeth. "Yes, there is."

After that they made love, and this time it wasn't a dream: for a moment all thoughts of captured colleagues were erased, and when she pressed her hand to his face so hard that he almost couldn't breathe, he forgot for several seconds to keep up his complaining and his usual running commentary. Then it was over, and they were each themselves again, and a little embarrassed, as if realizing how little they knew each other.

Leo gave his lecture in the ambassador's residence. Germans from industry, business, and the Foreign Service were there, the room was filled with men in suits and women with pearl necklaces, and the villa looked like the villa from the day before, and once again a city was spread out beneath them, and had it not been even hotter and the air terrible, you would have thought you were in the same place. Leo spoke extemporaneously, his head tilted back, his eyes fixed on the ceiling. He performed well, but Elisabeth could feel his anger. Had it been within his power, he would have condemned every one of them to death. Leo was not a well-meaning man. He didn't wish the best for people. This was so self-evident that she had to wonder once again why nobody seemed to pick up on it; and yet again she was forced to realize that people were bound up in their own preoccupations and worries, and registered so little of what was actually going on in front of them. When Leo finished there was applause, and then the previous day's reception repeated itself like a nightmare all over again: someone introduced himself as Mr. Riet, another as Dr. Henning, and then here came Mrs. Riedergott again, pale with excitement, because the ambassador was standing at her side, clapping Leo on the shoulder and asking where did he get his ideas from. He'd started Leo's last book in the plane en route from Berlin to Munich.

"Interesting," said Leo with an expression that matched his thoughts.

The ambassador nodded. "Your first time here?"

"The last."

"I see," said the ambassador.

"I'm going to kill you," said Leo.

"I'm so glad," said the ambassador. "I know you're in excellent hands." He smiled at Mrs. Riedergott and vanished into the crowd.

A line of people formed for everyone to shake hands with him and Elisabeth. They came from Wuppertal and Hannover, Bayreuth, Düsseldorf and Bebra, and a very straight-backed and desiccated gentleman came from Halle an der Saale. After a little while Elisabeth asked herself if the only people in the entire country were Germans.

"That," said Leo in the car, "is what becomes of art. Everything else is just illusion and propaganda. I've always said it. But I had no idea it was true!" She saw that he'd turned white. "All the work, all the struggle, all the worry, an entire life wrecked just for that. All for invitations from people who are brain-dead, all for handshakes, all so that the zombies have something to chatter about before they go to dinner."

In the front seat, Mrs. Riedergott suddenly turned round.

"No offense," cried Leo. "Dear Mrs. Riedergott, I was speaking in the most general terms."

That night, in the bathroom again, she finally got through to the secretary of state. Sitting on the toilet seat, she held the phone tight against her ear.

An awkward situation, he said in broken English. Really, there was nothing he could do. And even if he could, the efforts required would be considerable.

"Financial efforts?"

"Also financial."

That went without saying, she said. They also knew the value of his intervention and would be correspondingly grateful.

He couldn't promise anything, he said. He would be in touch again.

As she groped her way back into the dark bedroom, she

bumped into the night table. A glass fell to the ground and Leo woke up.

"Let's run!"

"What?"

"I'm not going to the reception at the International Chamber of Commerce tomorrow. I'm going to disappear, and that's that. We'll fly to the pyramids. I've always wanted to see them."

"Good."

"What are they going to do? File charges?" He hesitated. "Could they? Theoretically, I mean. Could they bring charges against me?"

"I don't think so."

"Yes, but *could* they?"

She sank down into her pillow. She was too tired to answer. She felt him looking at her in the darkness, and she knew he'd have liked to touch her, but she was too tired even to tell him that she was too tired.

In the morning, they left. A taxi to the airport, then the next plane up into the mountains. She had to spend the entire flight reassuring him that there wouldn't be consequences, that nobody would sue him, that nobody would end up in jail just for blowing off the German International Chamber of Commerce. Below them, the highest mountains she had ever seen slipped by, intensely green and covered in primeval forest.

"It's like the old days," he said, "when I skipped school."

"You never once skipped school."

"How do you know?"

"Did you?"

"Everyone did."

"Maybe, but you?"

He turned away to the porthole and didn't say a word till they landed.

The air on the upland plateau was so thin that it was hard to breathe and the heart raced with every movement of the body. Streets and houses glittered in an intense light that cut into them like knives, leaving no shadows, so that within minutes the skin was on fire. As their taxi honked its way through the crowds, she accessed a message from Moritz. Evidently the local government had intervened, he said, nothing definite, some rumors circulating that the hostages had been freed, others that they were dead. He promised to call as soon as he knew more.

They dropped their luggage at the first hotel they came to and hired a guide. He was tall and serious and taciturn. When Leo switched on his phone, there were seven messages from the cultural institute.

"I think there really is going to be trouble. What d'you think, are you sure they can't file suit against me?"

Ask me that one more time, she thought, and that's going to be it. One more time, and I'm on the next plane out.

But he didn't, probably because he couldn't catch his breath. They were climbing the slope behind their guide, hearing every hoarse gasp in his throat. Elisabeth's pulse was thundering, the sheer effort distracted her from her fear.

Their path took them through low grass, with spindly trees clinging to the rock here and there. Clouds had appeared out of nowhere, the air suddenly turned humid, the light fractured then diffused, and it began to rain.

They reached the pyramids in a torrential downpour. Thunderclaps echoed off the walls of the cliffs, lightning snaked across the horizon, and the only thing they could see in the mist were three stone peaks. Their guide was standing stock-still, water purling off his plastic poncho.

"Finally," said Leo, "none of this interests me. I write. I invent things. I really don't need to see stuff."

"And I don't want to turn up in a story."

He looked at her.

"Don't make me into someone. Don't put me in a story. It's all I ask."

"But it wouldn't be you in any case."

"Yes, it would. Even if it's not me, it would be me. As you very well know."

The rain stopped and minutes later the sun tore a hole in the clouds. The swaths of mist became translucent, and suddenly they were looking at the flights of steps that climbed the huge edifices. The valley below them seemed to sink into the abyss, and she had the sensation that the crest on which they were standing was rising slowly into the sky. Somewhere a stream was gurgling. She wondered why she had the urge to cry.

"This is where they killed people," said Leo. "Thousands of them. Every month."

FAME

"And the universe still retains that memory," said the guide impassively. "Close your eyes and you can feel it."

"How come you speak German?"

"Heidelberg. I studied ethnology. Nine semesters."

At that moment, her phone rang.

Rosalie Goes Off to Die

Of all my characters, she's the most intelligent. Almost seventy years ago, Rosalie was young and good at school, then she went on to qualify as a teacher and taught for four decades. She married twice and had three daughters, long since grown, now she's a widow, her pension covers her costs, and she's never been one to harbor illusions about things, so she wasn't surprised when her doctor told her last week that pancreatic cancer is incurable and she wasn't going to live much longer.

"I'm sure you want to know the truth," he said, looking at her as if she were a child who could be proud that an adult was taking her into his confidence. "The good news is that the bad pain doesn't come till the very end."

She really didn't have a difficulty accepting the situation. She didn't go through the famous seven stages: no rebellion, no denial, no slow struggle to arrive at an understanding—just a brief interval of incredulity followed by a night of the deepest sadness, then as soon as morning came, an Internet search for the Swiss association she'd heard about that helped people who wanted to hasten things along.

I'm sure you know this association really does exist; I didn't invent it, it's headquartered in a Zurich suburb, I'm not going to name it because my lawyer said not to. Several Swiss organizations offer assisted suicide; this one is the best known. If you haven't heard of it until now, pay attention; you can learn things even from a short story. You have to join the association, pay a not-negligible fee, send your medical records, which a doctor then examines to confirm that your condition is indeed terminal. After this is complete, you go there, install yourself in their only piece of actual real estate, the so-called death apartment: a room with a sofa, a bed, and a table, on which a gentle employee sets a glass of sodium pentobarbital. You drink it. Unassisted, and of your own free will.

When it comes to death, Rosalie is hard to impress. A cousin of her first husband's shot himself in the head without realizing how hard that actually is to do, and often people survive. The angle wasn't right and he vegetated for weeks, minus his lower jaw. Her friend Lore's sister tried it four times with sleeping pills. Each time she tried a higher dose, each time she came to, covered in her own excrement and vomit; our bodies are strong, and the will to live more powerful than we suppose in the dark nights of the soul. And Rosalie's nephew Frank, Lara Gaspard's brother, hanged himself eleven years ago. His neck turned black from the strangulation ligatures, and there were deep scratch marks on the ceiling. There's no harm in turning to the experts. So after a moment's feeling of revulsion, Rosalie reaches for the phone.

It's answered by a Mr. Freytag. He's polite, soft-spoken, and tactful, and he obviously has experience with these kinds of conversations.

I should really say that I've invented Mr. Freytag. I haven't called the association, I don't know who picks up the phone there and what is said. I wanted to find out, but a vague terror always stopped me, and I felt as if I were about to do something indecent, as if I were summoning up spirits for my own amusement. In addition to which, I'm not really the kind of writer who uses real facts. Others like to be meticulous and nail down every single tiny detail, so that some shop that one of their characters is wandering past has the exact right name in the book. This sort of thing leaves me cold.

"All very simple," says Mr. Freytag. This is the address, this is the fax number, please will she just send the medical records, a psychiatrist will then want to talk to her right away to verify that she's responsible for her actions. After that they'll fax her the membership agreements and as soon as she returns them, they'll be able to arrange a date. Is there any . . . for the first time he hesitates. Is there any particular urgency?

The doctor, says Rosalie, has spoken of a matter of weeks.

In which case, they'll put things on a fast track.

Mr. Freytag's voice doesn't waver, but is full of compassion. He's really good at it. And why not, thinks Rosalie, he could certainly earn more elsewhere, but this must be a real vocation. She even manages to feel a flash of gratitude.

FAME

In the night, she dreams in a way she hasn't done for years. Her blood pounds, her senses are so fevered that when she wakes up she's almost shocked at the very memory: so many people, so much noise, and the overexcited embraces. There are faces she hasn't thought about in more than fifty years, people who'd apparently vanished into oblivion, maybe she's the only person alive who still remembers them. How long ago it all was. It's really time for her to go.

And yet she can't resign herself totally to her fate. Which is why, as dawn is approaching, she turns to me and begs for mercy.

Rosalie, it's not within my power. I can't.

Of course you can! It's your story.

But it's about your last journey. If it wasn't, there'd be nothing for me to tell about you. The story—

Could take a different turn!

It's the only one I know. There *is* nothing else for you.

Whereupon she turns away and can't get back to sleep until it's light. There's nothing unusual about this, the last time she slept really well was more than twenty-five years ago.

The next days go by as if everything were normal and she still had time. Her terror slowly dissipates—or more accurately: it remains, but it loses its sharp edge and changes into a constant, dull pressure, not unlike the stomach pains that have been part of her existence for so long that she can now barely remember what it's like to have no pains at all. That is what life is when you're over seventy: a cramp here, a burning sensation there, a permanent sense of being unwell and stiffness in every joint.

45

She decides to say nothing to her daughters. They've been expecting her to die for a long time now, you have to be realistic. She's sure they've had detailed discussions about who will organize the funeral and where she's to be buried. They've dutifully begged her more than once to be sensible and move into a retirement home, but because Rosalie can still manage perfectly well on her own and retirement homes are expensive, their urgings have lacked conviction. So why burden them now, why have family reunions, tearful hugs and goodbyes? It will be so much better and cleaner if a sober letter from Zurich tells them that the long-anticipated event has now occurred.

She arranges to meet her two best friends, Lore and Silvia, for coffee and cake. There they sit, three old ladies, one afternoon in the best café in town, talking about their grandchildren. After a certain age, you only talk about your family. Politics and art become abstractions that no longer have anything to do with them and are left to the younger generation, and your own memories suddenly feel too personal to be shared. Which leaves the grandchildren. Nobody is interested in anyone else's but you listen, so that you'll have the right to talk about your own.

"Pauli's talking already," says Lore.

"Heino and Lubbi are in kindergarten," says Silvia. "The kindergarten teacher says Heino paints just wonderfully."

"Pauli's really good at painting too," says Lore.

"Tommi loves playing cops and robbers," says Rosalie. The other two nod, and although they've known Rosalie for thirty years, neither of them asks who Tommi is. There is no Tommi. Rosalie invented him, she has no idea why. Nor does she know if children today still play cops and robbers, she suspects it's anachronistic. She decides to ask her real grandson next time she sees him, then realizes that she's not ever going to see him again. Her throat tightens, and for a little while she's unable to speak.

To distract herself, she looks in the gold-framed mirror that's hanging on the wall. Is that really us? These little hats and crocodile handbags and eccentrically made-up faces, these fussy gestures and ridiculous clothes? What happened? Just a moment ago we were like everyone else, we knew how to dress, we didn't have these idiotic hairdos. That's exactly why, thinks Rosalie, everyone likes that eccentric detective Miss Marple—she's the absolute incarnation of unreality. Old women don't solve murders. They're not interested in the world, and they no longer have any desire to understand events. Every woman who hasn't got there yet thinks she's going to be different. Just as we did too.

They say goodbye to one another, for they've been sitting here for almost an hour and it's making them all nervous to have been away this long from home. As she stands up Rosalie looks at herself in the mirror once more: a heavy jacket, although it's summer, a waterproof rain hat, although it's not raining. And why is this purse so enormous, when there's almost nothing in it? Even her clothes signal that she's superfluous, a vestige, a human residue. You'll be next, she thinks as she gives Silvia and Lore each a kiss, wishes them luck with grandchildren and backaches, and walks across the street.

She doesn't see the car coming. In earlier days she would never have stepped blindly into the road, she would have paid attention without having to tell herself to do so. A horn blares, brakes scream, a red VW comes to a halt. The driver rolls down the window and yells something but she keeps walking, and now she hears a screeching noise from the other side, and a white Mercedes brakes so hard that it spins sideways; she's only ever seen something like that in a movie. Unmoved, she keeps walking. Only when she reaches the other sidewalk does her heart begin to thump, and she feels dizzy. Passersby have stood still. That's also a way things can work, she thinks, it's another way to shorten things, and it saves a trip to Zurich.

A young man seizes her elbow and asks if everything's okay.

"Yes," she says, "all okay."

He asks if she knows where she lives and how to get there.

A number of wicked replies occur to her, but she decides it's not the moment, and assures him she knows perfectly well.

Back home the light on her answering machine is blinking. Mr. Freytag is letting her know that her medical records have been approved. Her shock makes her realize that she's still been hoping they'd be rejected, that she'd be told that there's been an error and her case isn't incurable. She calls back, and a few moments later he's connected her to a very polite psychiatrist.

Unfortunately she has problems understanding his accent. What is it with the Swiss, she thinks, they can do it all, so why can't they manage to talk like normal people? She tells him things from childhood, names the American, French, and German presidents, describes the weather outside, adds fifteen and twenty-seven, and explains the difference between the concepts of optimistic and pessimistic, and skilled and unskilled. Anything else?

"No," says the doctor. "Thank you. Clear case."

Rosalie nods. During the additions she's forced herself not to answer too quickly, and take an extra moment or two so that he wouldn't think somebody's helping her. As for the explanations of words, she expressed herself as simply as possible. She was a schoolteacher, and knows from experience: the best thing is never to let yourself stand out. If your test results are too good, you're suspect and they think you've been cheating.

Now Mr. Freytag is back on the line. As time is pressing, she could come next week. "Would Monday suit you?"

"Monday," Rosalie repeats after him. "Why not?" Then she calls the travel agency and inquires about a one-way flight to Zurich.

"One-way is more expensive. Buy a round-trip."

"All right."

"What date for the return?"

"Doesn't matter."

"I don't recommend it. The cheapest tickets don't allow you any changes in bookings." The travel agent's voice sounds friendly and excessively patient, the kind of voice you only use when talking to elderly women. "Just a moment. When would you like to return?"

"I don't want to return."

"But you're going to want to come back."

"Maybe better to take a one-way ticket."

"I could also book it with an open return. But it is more expensive."

"More than a one-way flight?"

"Nothing is more expensive than a one-way flight."

"And that's logical?" asks Rosalie.

"Excuse me?"

"It's illogical."

"Dear lady . . ." He clears his throat. "This is a travel agency. We don't set the fares. We have no idea how they're established. My girlfriend works for an airline. She doesn't understand it either. I recently saw that a business-class fare to Chicago is cheaper than economy. The customer asked why, and I said, Sir, if I start asking questions like that, I'll come unglued. Ask your computer. I ask the computer too. Everyone asks the computer, that's how it goes!"

"Was it always this way with the pricing?"

His silence makes her realize he doesn't even want to think about this. She's often noticed that people under thirty aren't interested in why things become the way they are.

"So, I'll take the one-way ticket."

"Are you sure?"

"Absolutely."

"Business?"

She thinks it over. But it's not a long flight, why waste money? "Economy."

He mutters, types, mutters, types some more, and after a long-drawn-out fifteen minutes he issues her ticket. Unfortunately, he says, he can't issue it as an electronic ticket, the computer's acting up, nothing to be done. He'll have to have it delivered by messenger to her home. But that'll be even more expensive.

"Just do it," says Rosalie; she's really had enough.

She hangs up and it dawns on her that she no longer has a care in the world. The dripping tap she's been meaning to call the plumber about forever, the damp patch in the bathroom, the son of her neighbors who keeps staring up at her window so threateningly, as if intending to rob her—none of it matters a jot anymore, other people will take care of it all, or maybe no one will, it's over.

That evening she calls the one person she'd like to talk to about what she's going to do. "Where are you?"

"In San Francisco," says Lara Gaspard.

"The phone must cost you a lot, doesn't it?" How strange it is that these days you can reach almost anybody anywhere, without knowing where they are. It's as if space itself is no longer what it was. On the one hand it strikes her as spooky, on the other hand she's glad she can talk to her brilliant niece.

"No problem. What's going on, you sound strange!"

Rosalie swallows, then tells her. The whole thing suddenly strikes her as unreal and theatrical, as if it were someone else's story or someone had made the whole thing up. When she gets to the end, she doesn't know what else to say. Curiously, she finds this embarrassing. She stops talking, confused.

"My God," says Lara.

"Do you think it's a mistake?"

"Somewhere in there, there's a mistake, but it's hard to pin down. Are you going alone?"

Rosalie nods.

"Don't do that. Take me with you."

"Out of the question."

For a second or two, neither of them says a thing. Rosalie knows that Lara knows she would give way if asked more forcefully, and Lara knows that Rosalie knows, but Rosalie also knows that Lara doesn't have the strength for it, not now, not so abruptly and without any time to prepare, and so both of them behave as if there's nothing to be done and no argument to be had.

So they have a long conversation full of repetitions and interminable pauses, about life and childhood and God and the ultimate things, and Rosalie keeps thinking she shouldn't have made this call, that what she'd really like to do is hang up, but that it's really going to go on for some time because of course she absolutely doesn't want to hang up. At some point Lara begins to sob and Rosalie feels very brave and detached as she says goodbye, but then it starts all over again from the beginning and they talk for another hour. That was a mistake, Rosalie thinks afterward. You don't tell other people, you don't burden them with it. That's the mistake, that's what her brilliant niece meant. You do it alone or you don't do it at all.

The weekend goes by with a strange lightheartedness. Only her feverish dreams, filled with people, voices, and events, as if an entire universe buried inside her were trying to rise again to the light of day, show her that she isn't as serene as she believes herself to be in her waking hours. On Monday morning she gets ready to pack her suitcase. But she has to pull herself together, for it seems so strange and wrong somehow to be setting off on a journey minus any luggage.

In the taxi on the way to the airport, as the houses file past and the rising sun plays on the rooftops, she makes another try. Is there no chance, she asks me. It's all in your hands. Let me live!

Not possible, I say crossly. Rosalie, what's happening to you here is what you're for. That's why I invented you. Theoretically maybe I suppose I could intervene, but then the whole thing would be pointless! In other words, I can't.

Rubbish, she says. All babble. At some point it'll be your turn, and then you'll be begging just like me.

That's completely different.

And you won't understand why an exception can't be made for you.

The two things aren't comparable. You're my invention and I'm . . .

Yes?

I'm real!

Are you?

Trust me. It's not going to hurt. That much I can take care of, I promise. My story—

Excuse me, but I couldn't care less about your story. It's probably not even any *good*!

I'm furious and I say nothing, and to make sure Rosalie doesn't start up again, I have her arrive at the airport a few minutes later—the taxi has made unbelievable time, the streets have become a blur of color, and she's already getting out, no line at the check-in counter, no waiting to clear security, and she's sitting at the gate, surrounded by noisy children and people on business trips, and has no idea how all this happened. Our conversation has slipped into the back of her brain, she's no longer sure whether I actually said something or whether she invented my words herself.

The plane is late. All planes are always late, that's something not even I can do anything about. So Rosalie sits in the departure lounge. Sunlight filters softly through the windows. Until now she hasn't felt afraid, but suddenly she is rigid with terror.

At exactly this moment, things begin to move. The flight to Zurich is called, and as Rosalie stands up, a fellow passenger asks if she needs help. She doesn't, but why turn down the offer of a little support and friendliness? So she allows herself to be assisted on board.

Luckily, she has a window seat. She decides not to waste a moment, she's going to look out as if she could take it all with her. It's a fine thing to fly over the Alps one more time just before the end. The plane starts down the runway, engines screaming.

Rosalie wakes as the plane touches down and the force of the brakes presses her against her seatbelt. Her eardrums hurt. She rubs her forehead. Did she really . . . the whole way? She can't believe it. But out there the landing runway stretches away under a uniform gray sky. It's true, she's slept through it all.

"Are we really already there?" she asks her neighbor.

He shakes his head. "Basel."

"What?"

"Fog in Zurich." He looks at her as if it's her fault. "We had to land in Basel."

Rosalie stares at the back of the seat in front of her and tries to think. What is this? The unexpected twist that's meant to save her life? Have I intervened to interrupt her journey?

But Rosalie, I reply. You have cancer. You're going to die anyway. A break in your journey isn't going to save you.

It could turn into another kind of story, she says. I could discover life in the next two weeks. Do things I've never done before. It could be one of those stories about how nobody ever values the present enough and how you should always live as if it would be all over in the next few days. It could be a positive . . . what do they call them?

Life-affirming. It's called a life-affirming story.

So it could be one of those!

Rosalie, the airline will offer you two things. A connecting flight, but nobody will know when you'll be able to board, because the fog in Zurich is extremely thick, or a train ticket. The train would get you there on time. You'll take the train ticket. This isn't a life-affirming story. If anything, it's a theological one.

How so?

I say nothing.

But how so, she says again. What do you mean?

I say nothing.

"I beg you," says Rosalie's neighbor. "It's not so bad. You'll get to Zurich—it's not that far. There's no reason to cry."

At the door to the plane she's pulled herself together again. A man from the airline is handing out vouchers to the grumbling passengers. Rosalie does opt for the train, and because she looks frail and not very well, an employee is found to drive her to the station. Her train is already at the platform. "Mind the step," says the young man. "Mind, there's a gap. Mind the next step. Would you like to sit here? Mind the seat."

Very shortly the train is racing through a green landscape of hills and valleys. This time Rosalie is determined not to doze off.

She wakes as the train is stopping at some little provincial station. Fog hangs over the roofs of hideous houses. Out on the platform a child is whimpering while his mother next to him stares wildly as if she'd just trodden in a mound of turds. Rosalie rubs her face. Then the conductor comes onto the loudspeaker: there's been an accident, bodily injuries, please disembark!

"Someone's committed suicide," a man says cheerfully.

"Jumped in front of the train," says a woman. "That makes a mess of you. Nothing left!"

"Maybe a shoe," says the man. "It'll turn up miles away."

They all nod in concert, then they get out. A man helps Rosalie down onto the platform, and she stands out there in the drizzle. Not knowing what to do, she goes into the station buffet. A Madonna smiles down from the wall next to a general in black and white next to a mountain guide with a pickax. There are four Swiss flags in the room. The coffee is disgusting.

"Dear lady, do you wish to get to Zurich?"

She looks up. There's a thin man with horn-rim glasses and greasy hair at the next table. Rosalie has already noticed him on the train.

"If so, I could give you a lift."

"You have a car here?"

"Dear lady, there are many cars."

She's silent, nonplussed. But what does she have to lose? She nods.

"If you would be so kind as to come with me. I take it time is tight." In a grand gesture he pulls out his wallet and pays for her coffee. Then he goes over to the coat stand, takes a bright red cap that's hanging there, puts it on his head, and slowly adjusts it. "Forgive me if I don't assist you, but alas my back hurts. What is your name?"

She introduces herself.

He takes her hand and—she pulls back involuntarily—presses his lips to it. "Charmed!" He doesn't tell her his own name. He holds himself very straight, his movements are supple, and there's no sign that he has a bad back.

She follows him into the parking lot. He walks quickly

without looking back and she can hardly keep up with him. He stops first in front of one car, then another, his head to one side and his lips pursed.

"What do you think about this one?" he asks in front of a silver Citroën. "I think it will do the job." He looks questioningly at Rosalie. As she nods, disconcerted, he bends over and does something to the door, which springs open after a moment. He gets in and does something to the ignition.

"What are you doing?"

"Dear lady, won't you get in?"

Rosalie hesitantly sits down in the passenger seat. The engine starts. "Is this your car, or did you just . . ."

"Of course it's my car, dear lady! You wouldn't wish to insult me?"

"But the ignition! You . . ."

"A new patent, very complicated, why don't you tilt your seat back, it's not going to take long, even if I can't drive at top speed, too much fog and I don't want to expose you to the slightest danger." His laugh sounds like a bleat and Rosalie feels a shiver down her spine.

"Who are you?" she asks, her voice hoarse.

"A friendly fellow human being, dear lady. A seeker, a helper, a voyager. A shadow and a brother. As each of us should be to others."

They're already on the Autobahn. The guardrails glisten at the side of the car and the speed pushes Rosalie into her soft leather seat.

"The old riddle," he says with a sidelong glance at her face.

"Oedipus and the Sphinx. In the morning, four; at midday, two; in the evening, three. So profound, dear lady." He turns on the radio, alpenhorns groan, in the background someone yodels. He whistles along and bangs out the rhythm on the steering wheel, completely off the beat. "A thinking reed, most venerable lady, *un roseau pensant,* what else is man? I will take you to your destination, and all I ask in return, fear not, is absolutely nothing."

Get on and do something, she says to me. Spoil your story. Who's going to care, there are so many stories, it's not all about just one. You could make me better again, you could even make me young. It wouldn't cost you a thing.

She almost managed to coax me out of my reserve, but right now I'm preoccupied with other things: I'm really bothered that I have no idea who the guy behind the wheel is, who invented him, and how he got into my story. My plan involved a little boy and a bike, a motorcycle gang and a retired Colombian coffin maker. A little dog was also to be given a major role, largely symbolic. Twenty pages of drafts, a lot of them really good, that I can just as well throw away now.

They're already leaving the Autobahn, the first houses on the outskirts of Zurich appear: little gardens, advertisements for milk, more little gardens, schoolchildren with oversized knapsacks. Suddenly he hits the brakes, jumps out into the street, runs around the car, and opens Rosalie's door. "Dear lady!"

She climbs out. "We're here?"

"Yes indeed!" He makes an absurdly low bow, his arms hanging slack so that the backs of his hands brush the wet asphalt. He holds this pose for several seconds, then straightens up again. "Determination. Whatever projects you have planned, perform them with determination. Think about that." He turns and walks away with long strides.

"But your car!" Rosalie calls after him.

He's already disappeared around the corner, and the Citroën sits there abandoned, its blinkers going, and the door wide open. Rosalie squeezes her eyes, then focuses on the street sign, and realizes with a mixture of relief, incredulity, and anger that he's dropped her off in the wrong place.

She lifts her hand and stands there for a long time in the rain, getting wetter and wetter and feeling wretched beyond words. Finally a taxi pulls up. She gets in, gives the driver the correct address, and closes her eyes.

Let me live, she tries one last time. Your story. Forget it. Just let me live.

You're clutching at the illusion that you really exist, I reply. But you're made of words, vague images, and a few simple thoughts, and they all belong to other people. You think you're suffering. But nobody's suffering here, because nobody's *here*!

You and your clever words! You can stick them up your ass!

For a moment I'm speechless. I've no idea who taught her to talk like that. It's not who she is, it's a stylistic break, it spoils my prose. Please pull yourself together!

No, I won't. I hurt. One day it'll happen to you too, and someone will tell you that you don't exist.

Rosalie, that's precisely the difference. I do exist.

Oh yes?

I have a personality and feelings and a soul, which may not be immortal but it's real. Why are you laughing?

The driver looks round, then shrugs his shoulders, old people are strange and that's that. The windshield wipers are on high, rain is bouncing back up out of the puddles, people are staring out from under their umbrellas. The last journey, says Rosalie softly, and precisely because it's true, the thought rings both false and pathetic. It doesn't matter what kind of life you've had, she tells herself, it always ends in horror. And now all that remains is to let the minutes go by. There are approximately twenty left to her, each one filled with seconds; it's a long time. The clock will tick thousands of times more, the end is still unreal for now.

"We're here!" says the driver.

"Already?"

He nods. She realizes she hasn't changed any money, and has no Swiss francs. "Please wait. I'll be right back."

As she's getting out, she simply can't believe her last act is going to be cheating on a taxi fare. But life is such a mixed-up, impure business, and now she's no longer responsible. Here is the name board with all the buzzers, and on it, as if it meant something other than death itself, is the name of the association. She rings, the door immediately unlocks itself with a dull hum.

The elevator is ancient, the suspension cables above the car groan, and as she goes up, she understands that until this moment she'd never believed she would set foot in this house.

The car stops, the door glides open, and there appears out of nowhere, as if to prevent her from pushing the button that will take her back down again, a thin man with a center part in his hair. "Good day, my name is Freytag."

And now?

I know I should tell it all. Rosalie walking through the anteroom to the inner room in which the dying is done. The table; the chair; the bed, I should describe them, I should paint a picture of the battered furniture, the strange layer of dust on the little wall cupboard, the general air of a place that's both used and uninhabited, as if it were the home of shadows, not people. And of course the camera; I should mention the camera, installed to document that the terminally ill patients drink the poison themselves, that nobody forces them, the association has to cover itself legally. I should recount how Rosalie sits down and props her head on her hands, how she looks out of the window for one last sight of the endless foggy expanse of sky, how fear gives way to exhaustion, how she—here, please, and here, and again here—signs forms, and how the glass of poison is finally set down in front of her. I should describe how she lifts it to her mouth, I should conjure up the mixture of aversion and longing as she looks at the watery liquid, her brief hesitation, because she could still turn back and, even if for a matter of days, choose life with all its pain and all its adversities, but then she decides against this—she's come too far, she's too close to the threshold to turn back. I should also describe the last wave of her memories: games at the edge of a peaceful lake, the moist kiss of a motherly woman, her father behind the Sunday paper, the little girl who sat next to her at school, and a boy she hasn't thought about since back then, and the bird in a cage at her grandmother's that could enunciate several words quite clearly. Nothing, if truth be told, in the intervening seventy-two years, has ever fascinated her as much as that talking creature.

Yes, it could have made a really good story, a little sentimental, granted, but with humor to counterbalance the melancholy, the brutality offset by a touch of philosophy. I had worked the whole thing out. And now?

Now I ruin it. I tear the curtain aside, I become visible, I appear by Freytag's side at the door to the elevator. For a second he looks at me uncomprehendingly, then he turns pale and vanishes like dust. Rosalie, you're cured. And while we're at it, be young again. Start from the beginning again!

Before she can even respond, I've disappeared again and she's standing in the elevator that's grinding its way back downstairs and cannot grapple with the fact that a twenty-year-old woman is looking back at her out of the mirror. Slightly irregular teeth, hair a little sparse, neck too thin, she never was a beauty, but I can't give her that as well. Although, on the other hand—why not! It's not important anymore.

Thank you.

Ah, I say, exhausted, don't celebrate too fast.

She pulls open the front door and bounds out into the street on legs that no longer hurt. Her clothes look peculiar on her: a young girl dressed like an old woman. Because the taxi driver doesn't recognize her, he doesn't stop her, he's lost his fare and will still be standing here half an hour later, watching the meter keep ticking with rising concern, and finally banging on every door in the building. At the association they tell him that they were indeed expecting an old lady but that she hadn't bothered to keep her appointment. He will go off cursing and this evening will shovel down his wife's wretched cooking, even more taciturn than usual. It's long been in his mind to kill her, with a knife or his bare hands, but today's the day he decides to go through with it. But that's another story.

And Rosalie? She goes down the street, taking great strides, half unconscious with euphoria, and for a moment I feel I've done the right thing, as if mercy were all-important and one story less didn't matter. And at the same time, I have to confess, I have an absurd hope that someone someday will do the same for me. For like Rosalie I cannot imagine that I'm a nothing if I'm not being observed by somebody else, and that my only half-real existence ends the moment that that somebody takes his eyes off me—just as, now that I'm finally ending this story, Rosalie ceases to exist. From one moment to the next. Without any death throes, pain, or transition. At one instant an oddly dressed girl in a state of happy confusion, now a mere undulation in the air, a sound that echoes for a few seconds, a memory that bleaches itself from my mind and from yours as you read this paragraph.

What remains, if anything, is a street in the rain. Water

pouring off two children's ponchos, a dog over there lifting its leg, a yawning street sweeper, and three cars with unknown number plates rounding the corner as if they were coming from a long way away: out of another unknown reality or at least out of another story altogether.

The Way Out

I n the early summer of his thirty-ninth year, Ralf Tanner the actor began to feel he didn't exist.

From one day to the next, phone calls stopped. Friends of long standing vanished from his life, business plans collapsed for no good reason, a woman he'd loved insofar as he was capable maintained that he'd mocked her cruelly on the telephone, and another, Carla, suddenly surfaced in a hotel lobby to make the worst scene he'd ever undergone in his life: three times, she screamed, he'd stood her up three times in a row! People had stopped, grinning, to watch, a few of them had filmed it all on their cell phones, and already in the very moment Carla had hit him with all her strength, he knew that these few seconds would make it onto the Internet and eclipse the fame of his best films. Shortly after that, he was forced to part with his German shepherd because of allergies and in his distress he shut himself up to paint pictures that he didn't dare let anyone see. He bought albums of photographs of the designs on the wings of Central Asian butterflies, and read books on how to dismantle and reassemble watches without ever daring to try it himself.

He began to google his own name several times a day, corrected the Wikipedia entry on himself that was riddled with errors, checked the casting in his films in various databanks, and laboriously translated the opinions of participants in forums about them from Spanish, Italian, and Dutch. Absolute strangers got into fights in these forums about whether he really had split definitively with his brother years before, and he, who had never been able to stand his brother, read their views as if there might be a chance he'd find in them the answer to his existential crisis.

On YouTube he found the tape of a performance by a pretty good Ralf Tanner impersonator: a man who was almost his double—with a voice and gestures to match. On the right of the screen, the system offered a list of links to other videos connected with his name: clips from his films, two interviews, and of course the scene with Carla in the hotel lobby.

That evening he went out with a woman he'd been chasing for a long time. But when he was sitting opposite her, he suddenly found it impossible to pretend that her chatter interested him. The glances from people at the other tables, their whispering, and the direct staring, all disturbed him more than usual. As they got up to leave the restaurant, a man came up to ask for an autograph with the usual mixture of shyness and insistence.

"I only look like him, that's all," said Ralf.

The man eyed him suspiciously.

"It's my job. I do it onstage. I'm an impersonator!"

The man let them pass. The woman found his answer so funny, she was still laughing minutes later in the taxi.

That night, watching in the gray mirror as their two naked silhouettes merged, he wished himself with all his heart transported to the other side of its flat surface, and the next morning, as he listened to her breathing peacefully beside him he felt some stranger had wandered into the room by accident, and the stranger wasn't her.

He had long suspected that the act of being photographed was wearing out his face. Was it possible that every time you were filmed, another person came into being, a less-than-perfect copy that ousted you from your own presence? It seemed to him that after years of being famous only a part of him survived, and all he needed to be whole again was to die, and to be alone in the place he truly belonged: in films and in his myriad photographs. That body, the one that still breathed, felt hungry, and wandered around for no good reason, would cease to be a burden to him—a body that in any case bore little resemblance to the film star. So much work and so much makeup, so much effort and remodeling went into making sure that he really looked like the Ralf Tanner on the screen.

He called Malzacher, his agent, canceled the trip to the Valparaiso Film Festival, then set off to a discotheque called Looppool on the outskirts of town, where, according to what

he'd found on the Internet, there was going to be an appearance by famous actors' doubles. He told his chauffeur to wait
outside, and went in, feeling shyer than he had in years.
Someone wanted an entrance fee, but, when he saw Ralf's
face, waved him on in.

It was hot and sticky, the light harsh and flickering. Over
at the bar was a man who looked like Tom Cruise, Arnold
Schwarzenegger was clearing a path through the crowd at
the other end, and of course there was a Lady Diana in an
outfit straight from a discount store. People turned as he
went by, but their glances were brief and unfocused, slightly
indifferent. Diana now climbed up onstage and sang "Happy
Birthday, Mr. President"; there was obviously some mix-up,
but the crowd roared its approval. A woman smiled at him.
He looked back at her. She came toward him. His heart
began to thump, he didn't know what he should say. She was
at his side and then they were on the dance floor, her body
pressed close to his.

Shortly after that he found himself up onstage. People
stared up at him as he did his famous dialogue with Anthony
Hopkins from *I'm the Man in the Moon*. He did the Anthony
part really well, but stumbled a bit in his own replies. The
audience clapped and whooped, he jumped back down into
the room, and the woman he'd been dancing with whispered
in his ear that her name was Nora.

The owner of the discotheque tapped him on the shoulder
and gave him fifty euros. "That was okay, though not terrific.
Tanner talks differently, and he holds his hands sort of like

this." He demonstrated. "You look like him, but you haven't got his body language yet. Watch more of his movies! Come back next week."

As he and the woman stepped out onto the street, he panicked. He couldn't take her home with him. The moment she saw the house and the servants, she'd know that he wasn't who he claimed he was—or, rather, that he really was. He pretended not to see the waiting chauffeur, flagged down a taxi, invented something about a brother who was visiting right now; with a look that told him she didn't believe a word and assumed he must be married, she said her apartment was in a mess.

It was in fact small and extremely tidy, and Ralf Tanner spent the last night of his life there. It wasn't him but someone else who clasped Nora's body with a strength he'd never possessed before. In the early dawn she stroked his neck and told him he was wonderful. Many women had said this to him before, but he knew none of them had meant it.

Next day, under the name Matthias Wagner, he rented a furnished room in a rather drafty house not far from where she lived. The landlord looked at him with stupefaction, but Ralf explained that he moonlighted as an impersonator, and that apparently did it. He spent the whole week either there or with Nora, or walking up and down the street enjoying the fact that nobody turned to look, because word had spread around the neighborhood as to who he was and what he did.

Next time he appeared onstage at the Looppool, however, he didn't make such a good impression. As he stood there speaking his lines, he suddenly felt totally lost. Something was going wrong, he was tensed up, his voice sounded choked, and when he tried to remember how he'd held his hands in that particular scene, he no longer knew how it had been, what he'd felt and thought, all he saw was the image of himself on the screen. He could sense the audience's attention slipping away, and only his actor's instinct made him finish the scene.

Then he saw the other Ralf Tanner impersonator. He knew from YouTube that he'd achieved an impressive level of perfection, but the likeness was even more astounding in person. His handshake was firm and he had the penetrating look that Ralf recognized as his own from the big screen. He was tall and broad-shouldered and radiated strength, inner balance, and courage.

"You haven't been doing this long," he said.

Ralf shrugged.

"I've been doing it since his second film. At the beginning I was just an amateur, I was still working in the Lost and Found. Then his career took off and I handed in my notice." The man looked at him with narrowed eyes. "Are you going to make this your main job? It's hard—it takes lots of practice. To be able to interpret someone, you have to live with them. Often when I'm in the street I don't even notice that I'm doing Ralf Tanner. I *live* as him. I think like him, sometimes I stay in character for days at a time. I *am* Ralf Tanner. It takes years."

The owner of Looppool only wanted to give him thirty

euros this time. He hadn't really stood out, and the physical likeness wasn't there yet.

For a moment Ralf boiled with rage. He looked him straight in the eyes and the other man must have felt the force of a stare he knew from a dozen movies; he took a step back, looked down at the tips of his shoes, and muttered something incomprehensible. His hand slid into his pocket and Ralf knew that he was about to pull out another banknote. But then he felt his strength drain and the rage passed. He said he was just a beginner still.

"Okay." The man gave him a mistrustful look and the hand came out of the pocket empty.

"I'll really try," said Ralf. Something about this pleased him. Wasn't it proof that he was finally free?

No, he thought on the streetcar on the way to Matthias Wagner's place. Of course it didn't prove anything of the sort, it merely showed that self-examination disturbs the personality, deflects the will, and saps the mind; it proved that no one, seen clearly from the outside, resembles themselves at all. He got out at the next stop, waved down a taxi, and had himself driven home.

Once there he asked Ludwig, his valet, to draw him a bubble bath and prepared to listen while he waited to the voice messages on his cell phone. But there weren't any. Nobody seemed to have missed him. It was as if someone else had taken over all his personal affairs.

He spent the next day in restless distraction. His best friend Mogroll, the failed actor, had swallowed an overdose without warning. Intentional or unintentional, no one knew; he hadn't given any kind of a signal, hadn't talked to him, hadn't left any note. Ralf didn't understand it.

His personal trainer made him do his usual Wednesday push-ups and told him he had to work on his stomach muscles: there would be scenes in his next film where he'd be stripped to the waist, he mustn't be laughed at for no longer being young.

He checked the film forums to see if there was anything new about him, but when he read a posting saying that he had sawdust in his head and was as ugly as an ox, he gave up for the moment. Who wrote such stuff, and why? He talked to his agent, then with Brankner the director, who was embarrassingly obsequious. He knew that Brankner didn't reckon him a good actor but had to have him, because without his participation the movie would never get financed. Halfway through the conversation, Ralf hung up. He leafed through Miguel Auristos Blanco's *Peace, Reach Deep into Us* for awhile, then paced up and down looking at the flowers in the tall crystal vases that were suddenly scattered all around the house. He didn't like flowers, and had no idea how all the vases had got here. Had Ludwig bought them on his own initiative? He was getting stranger as he got older.

Ralf paused for awhile in front of the mirror on the wall, and watched his face become less and less recognizable by the second. Then he left the villa.

He breathed a sigh of relief when he reached Matthias Wagner's street. Supermarket right there, newsagent next door. The elevator car smelled of cooking. A fat woman greeted him casually. His room welcomed him like a lost refuge.

He watched TV and drank beer out of the can. A newscaster said something about war, the Near East, a visiting minister, tomorrow's weather. A housewife held up a colorful hand towel, then for some reason an elephant charged across a meadow, then Ralf Tanner appeared, steering a car through big-city traffic and talking to a blonde in the passenger seat. *"Time's running out and all these people will be turned to dust!"*

"But maybe," said the woman, *"we can stop it."*

Then in rapid succession came a series of explosions: a car flew into the air, then an oil platform—flames rolling decoratively over the sea—then an apartment building, hit so hard that a blizzard of glass shards flashed in the sun. Then Ralf Tanner's face again, and underneath, against a black background, the letters: *BY FIRE AND SWORD. In theaters now.*

What garbage, thought Ralf. Cringe-inducing.

That was when he realized he couldn't remember shooting it. And that he'd never even heard of the movie.

He channel-surfed for awhile, but the trailer didn't show up again. He went downstairs and across the street to the Internet café. The owner knew him already and pointed him, smiling, to one of the computers.

By Fire and Sword was listed on imdb.com. The film, which had apparently been reviewed very negatively in the papers the previous week, already had an entry in Wikipedia. In the MovieForum someone praised the intensity of his performance. But why had he gotten involved in such a film? Maybe, someone else replied, he needed the money, hardly surprising given the way he lived. A third person reported that Tanner was currently in Los Angeles, a fourth contradicted him: he was on a publicity tour in China. He'd also added a link, and when Ralf clicked on it, he found himself on the Web site of a Chinese newspaper. A large picture showed him grinning and shaking hands with two officials. He didn't know these people, he had never been to China. He paid and stumbled out into the harsh morning sun.

By Fire and Sword? Of course, said Nora, she'd seen it. And liked it. Who cared about the critics? She sighed. She'd worshipped Ralf Tanner since she was thirteen. She'd seen all his films.

"So that's why? Because I look like him?"

"Oh, you're not that like him. Maybe you should imitate someone else. You're good, but . . . he's not the right one for you."

His eyes slid to the mirror. There she was, and there he was, and suddenly he didn't know anymore which side the originals were on and which side the reflections. He ran his hand over her hair, murmured something to cover his confusion, and went downstairs to the streetcar stop.

In the streetcar, no one bothered him. He tried to see himself in the glass, but it didn't work, any more than it did in shop windows, there seemed to be no more reflecting surfaces to be found anywhere. On the edge of the sidewalk he saw two posters for *By Fire and Sword.* It wasn't till he reached the gate of the villa, all out of breath, that he realized his pockets were empty. He must have lost the key in all the turmoil. He pressed the bell.

"It's me," he called into the intercom. "I'm back early."

"Who?"

He swallowed. Then, fully aware that this response wasn't a good idea in the circumstances, he repeated, "Me."

The intercom was switched off. Thirty seconds later the front door opened: Ludwig came out and walked across the lawn, dragging his feet. Leaning against the grill, his weathered face peered through the bars.

"It's me," said Ralf for the third time.

"And who is 'me'?"

It took him a moment to understand that Ludwig wasn't trying to debate an abstract philosophical point, but that he didn't recognize him.

"I'm Ralf Tanner!"

"That'll surprise the boss."

"I'm back early."

"The boss came home hours ago," said Ludwig. "So please leave."

"This is my house!"

"We'll call the police."

"Can I . . . speak to the man who claims he's Ralf Tanner?"

"That's you."

"Excuse me?"

"The man who claims he's Ralf Tanner is you."

"Can I . . . speak to Ralf Tanner?"

Ludwig looked at him with a thin smile. "Ralf Tanner is a very famous actor. Hundreds of people want things from him. His phone never stops ringing. Do you think he's going to interrupt what he's doing to chat with you, because he's so glad you look like him?"

"Ludwig, surely you recognize me?"

"You know my name. Congratulations. So when did you hire me?"

He rubbed his forehead. What kind of a question was that? He was too taken aback to remember. Ludwig seemed to have been with him forever, that lumpy, lugubrious face his lifetime companion. "Can I speak to the others? Can you get Malzacher on the phone with me?"

"My dear man, let me give you some advice. Of course we can do these things. You can summon the entire household. Maybe you'll even get Ralf Tanner to come outside himself. But what would you have gained? Ridicule, mockery, an extremely unpleasant encounter with the police, and, if you keep this up, a charge of harassment. You're dealing with a star, and that means zero tolerance. He has to protect himself. I know he plays a large role in your life. You know all his movies, you accompany him and he accompanies you, he has no finer audience, but now you've reached a line you shouldn't try to cross. Go home. I'm an old man, I've seen a lot of you, and I don't want people to make themselves unhappy. You seem to be a nice guy. Pull yourself together!"

He felt dizzy. Opened his mouth and closed it again. Breathed in and out. Blinked in the sun.

"Are you feeling all right?" asked Ludwig. "Would you like a glass of water?"

He shook his head, turned around, and walked away slowly. All around him were villas, hedges, and high garden fences. There was a smell of mown grass. He stopped, then sat down on the ground.

What had happened? Had some imposter taken his place? It must be the impersonator he'd met in the Looppool; maybe the guy had seen through him and taken advantage of the moment to relegate him forcibly and completely into the role of a man named Matthias Wagner, spectator, imitator, and fan. A man who'd so submerged himself in the existence of a model who looked just like him that he'd come to confuse that other existence with his own. It happened. You could read about it in the newspapers. Pensively he took out his identity card, read the name printed on it as if for the first time, and put it back.

He looked up. On the other side of the street, the garden gate had opened. Ludwig and Malzacher came out, and between them, tall and well built, Ralf Tanner.

He couldn't remember ever looking that good himself. Whoever had chased him out of his own life, he was perfect at it, he was the right person for it, and if anyone had earned the right to Tanner's existence, it was him. What dignity, what charisma! A car drew up, Ralf Tanner opened the door, nodded to the chauffeur, and disappeared into the back. Malzacher got in after him, and Ludwig closed the gate.

As the car went by, Matthias Wagner leapt up and bowed,

but the windows were tinted and all he could see was his own reflection. The car had already passed him, turned the corner, and was gone.

He pushed his hands into his pockets and walked slowly down the street. He'd actually found the way out. He was free.

He paused at a bus stop but then changed his mind and continued on his way, he had no desire at this moment to use public transport, it was always a strange experience when you looked like a star. People stared, children asked stupid questions, and used their cell phones to take photographs of you. It could even be fun sometimes. It made you think you were someone else.

The East

How could she have known it was hot here? She'd imagined snow-covered steppes, swept by icy winds, whirling snows, nomads in front of tents, yaks, and campfires at night under huge skies canopied with stars. Actually, it smelled like one gigantic building site, cars blasted their horns, and the sun was scorching. A fly buzzed around her head. No cash machine anywhere. Yesterday at her bank, the teller had laughed at her: they didn't carry currencies like that, she'd have to change her money once she got there.

And here she was, enveloped in gas fumes, after an endless flight through the night. A hugely fat man in the next seat had snored all the way. Every time his hand fell into her lap, she'd asked herself why in the world she'd ever agreed to step in and make this trip. But she'd been curious to see this distant corner of the planet, and so she'd quickly decided to accept.

Not long afterward an air ticket arrived in the mail. The accompanying letter, in broken English, had a gold seal on it representing a flying bird or a sunrise or maybe a man wearing a hat. Then she had to go to the embassy—three rooms in a rental building on the outskirts—where a man in uniform wordlessly stamped a visa into her passport.

Her hair was already soaked with perspiration. She looked at her reflection in the dirty glass front of the terminal: a small plump woman in her mid-forties, looking absolutely exhausted. She had always been a person with a developed sense of curiosity, but tiredness undid her. Her favorite thing was to be at home, sitting in her cool study with the garden visible from the window and a cup of tea beside her. That's when she got her ideas, that's when she could concentrate, that's when she was in the right frame of mind to work out the tangled secrets that her melancholy detective, Commissioner Regler, had to solve. Her detective books sold well, she got fan mail from her readers. She loved her husband and her husband loved her. Her life was in order. Did she really have to burden herself with such trips?

A hand came down on her shoulder, and she spun around, startled. There was a man standing next to her in a stained suit. He was holding a piece of cardboard with her name written on it in clumsy letters.

"Yes, it's me!"

He indicated that she should follow him. She wanted to give him her suitcase, but he'd already set off and she had to run after him. They crossed the street, people yelled, cars honked, and when she got to the other side her skirt was splattered with mud. The car was parked across two spaces in the parking lot, the hood was dented, and it was filled with boxes. The trunk was jammed full of them, as was the backseat, and there was even one in front of the passenger seat, so that she had to lift her feet and hold her purse in her lap. She wondered what the man could be transporting. When she moved to fasten her seatbelt, he shook his head and swore; obviously he considered it an insult to his capabilities. She gave in.

He talked to himself softly the whole way. Once he braked sharply, rolled down the window, and spat onto the street. "You business," he said. "Kill why?"

She smiled to show she didn't understand.

"Everything," said the man. "Foam. Lorry?"

She shrugged.

"Hobble," said the man. "Hobble grease. Why?"

She smiled awkwardly.

"Why?" The man banged on the window. "Grease, the hobble why!"

She lifted her hands and shook her head, but that only made him angrier. He pointed first in one direction, then in another, hit the dashboard, yelled, and seemed to have lost any awareness of the traffic. Finally he braked in front of a building. A guard was leaning against the glass door, a flag flapping above him in the wind. The hotel. They got out.

Cranes towered up against a milky sky. The ground was littered with tin cans, twisted pieces of wire, and shards of glass. The guard yanked open the door and she went in.

The front hall was made of marble, with a fountain in the middle with the water turned down to a trickle. The woman at the reception desk spoke no English. After the driver had harangued her for awhile, she wordlessly handed over a key.

But the room at least seemed habitable. The bed was soft and clean, the faucets in the bathroom worked. Outside you could see a dozen high buildings and factory chimneys. Just as she was about to unpack, the phone rang.

"Downstairs," said a woman's voice in uncertain English. "Now."

She wanted to ask a question but the woman had already hung up. She hastily changed out of her sweat-soaked blouse into a fresh one, dutifully picked up her notebook, and took the creaking elevator down.

A number of men and women were sitting in a semicircle in the front hall on folding chairs. In the middle was a woman wearing a uniform.

"Am I the last?"

The woman asked who she was.

"Maria Rubinstein. I'm Maria Rubinstein."

The woman stared at a sheet of paper, then shook her head.

"I'm here instead of Leo Richter. They sent me his ticket. I'm replacing him."

Leo Richter, said the woman. He was on the list!

"He's not coming. I'm here in his place."

The woman made a disdainful gesture that obviously implied that nobody could understand what went on in foreigners' heads. She pointed to an empty chair. Maria sat down and the woman made a short speech. This prominent delegation of the world's best travel journalists had been invited by the government of the fatherland to report to all nations on its beauty. They would lack for nothing, their every wish would be granted. They would even meet the vice president, the festivities would have no end. And now, the welcome banquet!

She led them into an adjoining room. There was a long table with bowls of cold potatoes. Between them there were platters of fatty roast pork in mayonnaise.

As Maria established very quickly, nobody here was a travel journalist. There were two cultural editors and three trainees who'd been sent because nobody on the staff wanted to come here. Then there also was a science editor from *La Repubblica* and a friendly man who wrote articles on wild birds for the *Observer*. An older woman had worked for German Radio before her retirement, and her colleague was only here because there were workmen in her apartment. As soon as dinner was over, Maria went to bed.

She slept badly. The distant sound of machinery woke her again and again. When she got up with a raging headache, she realized she'd forgotten the charger for her cell phone. Dejected, she sent her husband a text message. *I miss you.* There was no reply. She felt very far away from everything.

In the lobby she inquired about a charger. The receptionist stared at her silently in a state of incomprehension. One by one her colleagues appeared. Most of them were pale and had slept badly. "That mayonnaise," said the man from the *Observer*. "Lethal!"

FAME

A bus drove them for two hours on potholed streets. As Maria came to out of her drowsy half sleep, they were in front of a factory building. Workers had gathered and were singing. The guide pointed to a conveyer belt. It was impossible to tell what was being made here. A woman brought a plate with roast pork still in its rind. Everyone took a piece hesitantly. The choir sang again, then they drove back. When they reached the hotel, night had already fallen.

Every day that followed was the same. They were driven to a swimming pool in an unlit concrete hall. The water looked cold and smelled of chemicals. The man from *La Repubblica* asked if he could swim a lap, and the guide said it was impossible. They were driven to a sewage plant, they were driven to a drilling tower in the swamps of no-man's-land, and an industrial bakery, they were driven to a place where eighty years before there had still been a nomads' camping ground. Once these people had laid waste to everything, the guide said, with sabers and cudgels and whips, they had ridden out to rape women and burn fields until it was decided to make short shrift of them and they were slaughtered down to the last man. They were driven to the parliament building where several hundred deputies who all belonged to the same party sang the national anthem for them, hands on their hearts and their eyes uplifted to the portrait of the president.

They were driven to an electrical transformer which for some reason was without electrical power, they were taken to a primary school where children in uniform were waiting outside the door and sang them old folksongs for two hours while the sun burned and the flies attacked. The retired editor from German Radio fainted and had to be carried into the bus. The singing went on for another hour before a deputation of schoolgirls handed around roast pork with mayonnaise that they'd made themselves. They were driven to the university, where a professor with a wild beard gave a lecture in almost impenetrable English about the brilliant perspectives and future opportunities of the country. As far as Maria understood, he was talking about steel and oil and the president, and the place smelled of ammonia and the stench from the building sites drifted through the open windows. When he'd finished, they served roast pork.

They were driven out onto the steppes. The bus stopped. They got out. Here, there was nothing.

The grass undulated gently. The sky soared, two little frayed clouds its only decoration. There was no stench, there was no smell, the air was clean. The wind was soft. The plain stretched away to the horizon with nothing to interrupt the eye. A skein of birds floated by. A dragonfly flew up, wheeled in a circle, its wings buzzing, then sank back down into the grass.

As they drove on, it seemed to Maria that they hadn't moved from the spot; no matter where you looked, nothing changed, in any direction. She closed her eyes. For the moment she was sleeping better on the bus than she did in the noisy hotel.

That evening she switched on her cell phone and called her husband. On the sixth attempt it worked and suddenly she heard his voice.

"Oh God," she said. "If you only knew."

"The food?"

"Ah."

"The people?"

"Ah again."

Neither of them said anything for a few seconds. She knew he understood.

"The flowers?" she asked finally.

"I water them every day."

"The garbage?"

"Already took it out long ago. Is it freezing there?"

"It's boiling. And the mosquitoes are appalling!"

"God!"

They fell silent again, then it occurred to her that she needed to spare the battery. The thought that the phone could actually die made her panic-stricken.

"I'll be back soon," she said.

"Do you have anything against mosquitoes?"

"Excuse me?"

"Bug spray?"

"Doesn't exist here."

"Well you could—"

She never did find out what suggestion he was going to make. The connection failed and all she heard was the busy signal. The battery was almost flat. She sighed and switched off.

The next day was the last. They were driven to a little provincial town far out on the steppes; from there they would be delivered to a military airfield the following morning. A government plane would take them to China, where they would connect with a regular flight that would take them home.

They were shown a building site. Maria had no idea what was being built, but it must be important, because each of them had to take a spadeful of bad-smelling soil and throw it onto a mound. They all looked exhausted: some of them had lost weight, many were pale, one of the trainees had been smitten with a strange form of acne, the man from *La Repub-blica* was limping, and the old lady from German Radio just sat on the bus with her head in her hands. Shortly after this they were taken to another building site where the same thing happened all over again, then to a military barracks where the company was drawn up outside. The national anthem was played. Flags waved. There was roast pork in mayonnaise. After that—it was nighttime now—they were driven to the hotel.

A little man handed out the keys. Maria was the last in line, and when it was her turn there were no keys left. Someone had miscounted. The hotel was full.

The guide screamed at the receptionist, the receptionist seized the phone and screamed, hung up, dialed another number, screamed, hung up, and stared at her truculently.

"Then I'll just share a room with someone," said Maria.

"No problem," said the woman from German Radio. "Come in with me. We're grown-ups."

Impossible, said the guide. It just wasn't done. The country was full of hotels and all of them were excellent!

And so Maria found herself sitting alone in the bus. For half an hour they drove down pitch-dark streets, until finally they came to a halt outside a tall building. Children were loafing around on the sidewalk. And old women were selling pumpkins.

The hotel, said the guide, wasn't open right now but they would make an exception for Maria, she would be given a room. Tomorrow morning she must be downstairs on the street at seven twenty-five sharp, for the bus to pick her up and take her to the airport.

"For sure?"

The guide looked at her expressionlessly.

The elevator was broken, a bearded man led her up the stairs to the seventh floor. Why did she have to go up so many floors when the hotel was empty anyway? Finally she reached her room, sweating and out of breath. It smelled of chemical cleaners. The wardrobe wouldn't close, the television didn't work, the curtains were creased. On the wall hung a piece of paper covered in Cyrillic lettering. What did it say? Doesn't matter, thought Maria, this is almost over.

She lay awake for a long time staring at the ceiling. In the distance she could hear traffic. She checked her alarm clock three times. Although everything seemed to be working, she couldn't get to sleep for fear it wouldn't ring.

The next morning, she was already heading downstairs at five past seven. She set her suitcase down in the front hall and sat down in an ancient fake-leather armchair. There was no one to be seen. She waited. Ten minutes went by. Twelve. Fifteen. She went out onto the street. Cars were driving in the pale morning light, but there were no pedestrians in sight. She checked her watch again. It was now three minutes past the half hour. Then four minutes. Then four and a half minutes. Suddenly, with a shock, she saw it was twenty to eight. Quarter to eight. Ten to. It was five to eight. She switched on her phone, but had no idea who to call. There was no contact number in case of emergencies. The group had always stayed together, so nobody had thought of such a thing.

Steady, she thought. Steady! Someone would notice she was missing, the others would raise the alarm, the plane would wait. She went back into the front hall and sat down.

After a minute she got up again and went out to the street. She stood there, her heart thumping, for two hours. The heat came, tentatively at first, then in increasing waves. The crowds thickened around her, and the flies too were beginning their day. She went back into the hotel several times, but there was no one to be seen, the reception desk remained empty, and calling, banging, and yelling did no good. Who was the bearded man from yesterday, and where could he be now? Then she went back outside and stared at her watch.

Around midday she climbed back up to her room. The building did seem to be totally empty. In the early afternoon she dozed off, but cold fear woke her again almost immediately. For awhile she stood at the window, then she sat at the table, drumming her fingers and staring at the wall. She went into the bathroom and cried for awhile. Then she stood at the window again and watched the light fade. Was it possible that the others hadn't noticed she was missing, or that they'd accepted some threadbare explanation to avoid any delay in their own departure? Something told her this was perfectly possible. She lay down on the bed. It was only now that she noticed she was hungry.

But she couldn't go anywhere! If anyone went looking for her, this is where they would come. She switched on the phone and tried to reach her husband. She couldn't get a connection. After the third try she switched it off again, so as not to use up the very last of the battery.

Strangely enough, she slept a deep, dreamless sleep and when she woke up, for a few seconds she felt rested and relaxed. Light was coming through the window and motes of dust were dancing in the sunbeams. Then she remembered. The fear hit her like a whiplash. Hastily she got dressed.

After an hour of searching she knew that the building really was totally deserted. She had gone through every floor, calling and knocking on every door. The phone on the reception desk seemed to work, but she didn't know what numbers she had to dial to get an international connection; no matter what she tried, she heard the same harsh whistle in the receiver. When another three hours had gone by and nobody had appeared, she decided to leave. She had to find somebody who could help her.

The heat was worse than the day before. Her clothes soon stuck to her body, sweat ran down her face, and she was so weak from hunger that she could barely carry her suitcase any longer. In a shop filled with canned goods and flat circles of bread mummified in plastic wrap, she tried to buy a slice of cake and a bottle of water. She had reached the cash register before she realized she had no local currency, only euros, a few dollar bills, and her credit card. The owner refused all of them. Tears came to her eyes. In helpless pantomime she tried to make clear to him that ten dollars were worth far more than the few coins he wanted from her. He shook his head. She picked up her suitcase and went out.

In the third shop, someone was finally prepared, in exchange for twenty dollars, to give her three lumpy, doughy objects stuffed with pork and a bottle of water. With relief she leaned against a wall and ate and drank. She immediately felt nauseous and heavy in the stomach, but as she'd felt the same all week, she didn't worry too much about it.

As she set off again, she noticed people turning around as she passed. Men gave her amused looks, children kept pointing at her and calling out things until they were pulled along by their mothers.

She spoke to a policeman. He turned to look at her, his eyes small and hostile. She tried English, French, German, and even her halting classical Greek, learned many years ago for a seminar on Aristotle at university. She tried pantomime, folding her hands in a pleading gesture. Finally he stretched out a hand and said something. She didn't understand, he repeated it, this went on for some time until she realized he was asking for her passport. He took it, leafed through it, looked at her sharply, and screamed a sentence she didn't understand.

"Please help me!"

With an impatient movement he motioned for her to come with him. The police station, only one street away, was small and dirty. For some incomprehensible reason her travel bag and her watch were taken away. Maria was made to sit in a tiny room and wait.

For a long time, nothing happened. The clock on the wall had stopped, the hands didn't move. Maria lay her head on her arms. Time seemed to stand still. She was dizzy with boredom. At some point the door opened, a man in uniform came in and spoke to her in English.

"My God, finally! Please help me."

Her passport, he said, was old.

"Excuse me?"

The sign in the passport. Old.

She didn't understand.

He looked up at the ceiling and thought for awhile, until he found the right words: her visa had expired.

"Well yes of course! I was supposed to fly out yesterday, but nobody came to collect me."

She couldn't stay here without a visa.

"But I don't *want* to stay here!"

Not possible. Not without a visa.

She rubbed her eyes. She felt utterly weak. Then she explained the whole thing as slowly and clearly as she could. She said she was a guest of the government, she described the delegation of journalists and their tour. She was a guest of the state! And then they'd obviously forgotten her and the plane had left without her.

He said nothing for awhile. Loud laughter was audible

from the next room. Here without visa, he said finally, not permissible.

She began at the beginning again. She recounted the whole thing all over again: delegation of journalists, tour, guest of state, collect, forget. Before she could finish, he went out and slammed the door behind him.

It must be dark outside now. At some point Maria knocked on the door. A policeman opened it and took her to a filthy toilet. Back in the little room she wanted to try to see if her phone would get a connection, but, like everything else, it was in her bag. She wiped her nose with the back of her hand. How long had she been here? It could be hours or days. Then the door flew open, and the policeman who'd interrogated her came back into the room.

Everything false, he cried. Everything lies! He threw a sheet of paper down in front of her, and on it, in Cyrillic letters, she recognized the names of everyone in the group. The colleague from the *Observer,* the one from *La Repubblica,* the trainees, the woman from German Radio—and Leo Richter.

"He didn't come," she cried. "This one! Him!" With a trembling finger she pointed to his name. "Canceled. I for him!"

The policeman seized the paper, stared at it, threw it back on the table, and said her name wasn't on it anywhere.

"I'm here for him! Leo Richter! He canceled!"

She was not, he said, on the list.

She begged him to call the guide. She would recognize her, she would explain everything.

Nothing moved in his face.

"The leader of our group! Or an ambassador? Couldn't you call the German ambassador?"

He thought. This time he'd understood her. Germany had no embassy here.

"And England, France, America?"

China. There was a Chinese embassy in the capital. Probably a Russian embassy too. But without a valid visa she couldn't get on a train and go there. It was forbidden.

Maria tried to control herself but she couldn't anymore, and burst into tears. Her body was racked with helpless sobs, and she cried until she could no longer breathe. She was surprised she didn't pass out. But she remained conscious of the room with the table, the clock on the wall, and the indifferent policeman, and finally she calmed down again. Wiping away her tears, she asked to be allowed to make an international call.

Hard, he said. Connections bad. This not the capital.

"Please!"

Besides which he no can help her. She have no visa. She illegal here!

He went out and she heard loud voices from the next door. They were obviously fighting about what to do next. Her strength had left her; none of it seemed real anymore and she laid her head back down on her arms.

She woke up when someone shook her shoulder. The policeman standing there was the one who'd just—or maybe the day before, or who knew when—taken her to the toilet. Her bag was set next to her on the floor. He led her out, through the adjoining room and onto the street. It must be early afternoon, because it was blazingly hot. He made a sign. She didn't understand. He did it again. She realized she was supposed to go.

"No!" she cried. "Please! Help me!"

He looked at her. His face wasn't unfriendly, even almost sympathetic. Then he spat on the asphalt.

"My watch," she said hoarsely. "You still have it."

He banged the door shut behind her.

She took her bag and set off. Gradually it dawned on her: the policemen hadn't known what to do with her, they didn't want any difficulties, and so they'd simply sent her away. She was probably lucky they hadn't locked her up or killed her.

She pulled out the phone, dialed, and heard a voice saying the number she was dialing was not in service. She dialed again, heard it again, dialed yet again. The battery light was flashing red. When she tried the fourth time, her husband answered.

"Oh God, finally! You can't imagine what's happened!"

"Yes?"

"They left without me. Nobody will help me. Please call the Foreign Ministry!"

"Yes?"

"You have to put pressure on them, tell them it was an official invitation. Go to a newspaper. It's serious, it's really serious!"

"Yes?"

"Hello?"

"I can't hear a thing. Who's this? I can't hear a thing!"

"Maria!" she screamed. People turned around to look at her. A wrinkled woman grinned a toothless grin.

"Maria, is that you?"

"Yes, it's me! Me!"

"Please call back. I can't hear a thing." He hung up.

She tried again. When she pushed the redial button, the screen was blank. The battery was dead.

She had no idea how long she wandered through the town. Her hair was glued to her head, her hands ached from the weight of the suitcase. It wasn't until she wanted to eat something and searched in her bag for her wallet that she realized the policemen had taken this too.

She leaned against a house wall and stared blankly in front of her. Then she went on. Suddenly the painful weight wasn't painful anymore, and she realized she'd put down the bag and left it somewhere. She turned around. There it stood, a small thing of gray leather, looking so abandoned that Maria felt a pang of sympathy. She turned the corner, walked around the block, and when she got back to the spot, the bag was no longer there.

Lie down on the ground, she thought. Collapse, just be there: someone would take her to a hospital, and they'd have to pay attention to her.

But no, that wasn't true. If she was lying on the ground, people would just leave her there. Besides, the street was filthy, the asphalt cracked all over the place, she could see brownish water running along the cracks, and there was broken glass everywhere. This was not an ideal place to have a breakdown.

She stopped. There, behind a shop window—books! Not many, but if she was deciphering the script correctly, there was a Pushkin edition and something by Tolstoy among them. Where there were books, there might be someone who spoke other languages, maybe they'd understand her. Excited, she went in.

It was a grocer's. On the shelves behind the counter were piles of canned goods and boxes of all sizes with Chinese lettering. And indeed there were a few books. A little man was looking at her with narrowed eyes.

"Do you speak English?"

He spoke neither English nor French nor German nor Greek, nor did he understand her sign language. He stood there motionless, watching her, his polite smile never wavering.

She pulled out a stool. The sun had been so fierce; she needed to sit down for a moment. And she was so thirsty. As soon as she made a goblet of her hands and lifted them to her mouth, he understood: he reached for a plastic container and poured her a glass. A few days ago the glass and the little brown filaments swimming in the water would have disgusted her, but now she drank it greedily. Then she sat for awhile, hunched over, her elbows propped on her knees. The little man waited at a respectful distance.

When she raised her head, she saw, between two Auristos Blanco titles, something she knew. She got to her feet and pulled it out. A cheap cardboard binding, garish red. Her name in Cyrillic script over a title she couldn't read, but she knew it was *Dark Rain,* her most successful novel. Under the title was a photograph of a man in sunglasses and a wide-brimmed hat. This was how her Russian publisher had represented Commissioner Regler, her melancholy detective opposed to all forms of violence. How ridiculous she'd found it, how she and her husband had laughed over it!

She turned it over; no author photograph. She showed it to the little man, tapped her finger on the book, then pointed to herself.

He smiled, baffled.

She pushed it back onto the shelf. "You're right. It doesn't matter. It doesn't change anything."

He bowed.

She thanked him for the water and left.

She came to a marketplace. It smelled of sheep and rotten fruit, and the stalls were in the process of being dismantled. She went up to a big woman in an apron who looked friendlier than the others, and pointed to her mouth and stomach. The woman gave her a hunk of bread. It tasted good; admittedly a little bitter, but it gave her strength. The woman also gave her a water bottle, and after she'd drunk from it, she felt almost restored.

The woman was very wrinkled, several of her teeth were missing, and one of her eyes was half closed, the eyelids drooping to one side. She said something Maria didn't understand. Then she hoisted a crate of potatoes and indicated to Maria that she should help carry them.

Together they hauled the crate across the street to where

an old man was waiting by a tractor, and heaved it up onto the trailer. The woman squatted down behind it and gestured to Maria to do the same.

Bathed in gasoline fumes, they set off judderingly. The town soon disappeared and the steppe spread out in the twilight. The air turned cooler. For a long time a dragonfly flew beside them. The woman's head nodded with every stroke of the engine, she seemed to be sleeping with her eyes open. The sky was empty, not a bird to be seen. Night fell.

When they reached the house, it was dark. Maria jumped down from the trailer; the ground was so muddy that she sank in up to her ankles. The house was built of weathered planks, the roof was corrugated iron; inside it smelled musty, and as the old man lit two torches, she saw a mouse run off. Outside the woman was working a rusty pump. She brought in a tin pan full of water, set it down, pointed to the wooden floor, the pail, and the floor again. Then she gave Maria a cloth.

While she cleaned, Maria tried to think. She would have to live here for a year, maybe two, no search party would find her, no envoy from the Foreign Ministry would suddenly appear to free her. She would have to stay and work until she learned the language. If these people paid her something, she'd set some money aside. At some point she'd be able to make her way to the capital. There she'd find someone who could help her. She wouldn't be stuck here for an eternity; she was better equipped than these people; she'd come out of this.

In no time her back was aching, her arms weren't used to

the exertion, and it looked to her as if the floorboards were actually getting dirtier as she worked. She sobbed quietly. The woman sat in her chair and peeled potatoes. The old man squatted on a wooden bench, staring blankly into space.

When she'd finished, the floor looked exactly the way it had before, but the woman gave her another piece of bread and even some meat. After she'd eaten it, she went out to the pump and washed her face and hands. All of a sudden, it was freezing cold. An animal howled in the distance. The sky was full of stars.

The woman showed her the mattress on which she was allowed to sleep. It was surprisingly soft, there was just one place where a rusty spring had poked its way through, and she had to curl up to prevent it jabbing into her back. For a moment she thought about her husband. Suddenly he seemed a stranger, like someone whom she'd known long ago, in another world or a past life. She heard herself breathing, and realized that she was already asleep, looking down on herself in a dream. With astonishing clarity she knew that such moments were rare and she must be very careful. One false move and there would be no way back, her former life would be gone, never to return. She sighed. Or perhaps she only dreamed the sigh. And then, finally, she lost consciousness.

Replying to the Abbess

Miguel Auristos Blanco, the writer venerated by half
the planet and mildly despised by the other, author
of books on serenity, inner grace, and the wandering journey in quest of the meaning of life across hills, mead-
ows, and valleys, paced ceremoniously into his study in the
front of his penthouse apartment in a skyscraper high above
the glittering coastline of Rio de Janeiro. A blinding light
came off the sea; on the other side of the bay, first clearly, then
in patches of gray shadow, the shapes of the mountains stood
out, their slopes edged with the favelas. Miguel Auristos
Blanco shaded his eyes with his hand, the better to see his
desk: two gold pens, seventeen well-sharpened pencils, a flat
keyboard in front of a flat screen, and in the filing tray the
perfectly aligned stack of pages of his new manuscript, *Ask
the Cosmos, It Will Speak*. Only one chapter still to write after
the entire opus had written itself with the same effortlessness
over the previous four weeks as had all his previous books;

this one was about the faith and the trust that were engendered by the gestures and rituals which served to express them, and not, as was so often supposed, the other way around: if you were true to someone, you would begin to love them, if you helped a friend, you would become more honest with yourself, if you made yourself attend a Mass, you would find that it ceased to be a blind ritual and gradually revealed the existence and nearness of a Supreme Being watching over you.

Miguel Auristos Blanco didn't invent these things, they came of their own volition and found their way into the manuscript without any help from him while he sat there watching with restrained curiosity as his typing fingers put line after line up onto the shimmering white screen, and when he stood at the end of a working day, and—like now, for instance—blinked as he watched the sun go down, he was no less exalted and edified than all of his seven millions readers were about to be.

He sighed. With a quick movement of the left hand, on whose middle finger a small tapered sapphire gleamed, he stroked first his moustache and then his thinning hair. As always when he came back from the toilet, he felt both comforted and prey to a vague melancholy. He was spending a great deal of time on the toilet these days; his doctor had told him recently that he would have to have a prostate operation soon. Miguel Auristos Blanco tilted his head, licked his lips, and heard himself give a faint sigh again. He was wearing bespoke shoes of highly polished chestnut leather, white linen trousers, and a white silk shirt open to the third button. His gray chest hair was more sparse than it used to be, but his body, at sixty-four, was athletic, with the flat stomach only to be seen on people who have a personal trainer: every day, under the watchful eye of Gustavo Monti, the former Olympic gold medalist, he trotted on a groaning, rolling treadmill about which he had once written a little book on the affirmation of uniformity, the changes within continuity, and the gentle swaying of the spirit as it moves between exhaustion and concentration. (Naturally he used the apparatus only when he was here in the city. When he was in his country house close to Parati or in his Swiss chalet on the other side of the ocean, he moved in a trance every morning through the cool and the air, his attention focused on his own breathing and on the slowly building warmth of the new day.) The book wasn't one of his most successful, but he loved it so much that he often read it to himself before he went jogging.

He hesitated. Had he sighed again? In a sudden impulse, he held his arms wide; it was as if he were feeling a sea wind. But of course he knew it was only the breeze from the almost-silent air conditioner.

As he walked toward his desk, his fingertips delicately removed a flower seed from his sleeve, flicked it away, and he watched the tiny silky fluff float away, sparkle in a ray of sunshine, and vanish into the air. Then he sank into his desk chair: upholstered in leather, supple, following the contours of his back exactly, made by the best chair-maker in São

Paulo. For a few seconds he rocked, the tips of both index fingers against his nose, his thumbs between his lips pursed in thought. Then he opened the second drawer from the top and took out, as he did so often, a pistol that was lying inside ready: a Glock, barrel length 114 millimeters, caliber 9 millimeters, never used, for which he had not only a permit but also authorization to carry it loaded.

Miguel Auristos Blanco liked weapons, if only as toys, he had never used one in anger. On his sun-spangled lawn in Parati he regularly did target practice, sometimes with bow and arrow, sometimes with a light hunting rifle in front of the patiently receptive round board. *A Steady Hand Makes a Calm Spirit* was the title of the book in which he elaborated on how when shooting one must become One with the target, so that success is no longer a concern, and for this very reason, one enters a paradoxical state that oscillates between tension and detachment and hits the bull's-eye. It was not his strongest work, and only years later did he realize with a certain shock that it paraphrased almost in its entirety a very famous book about Japanese archery that he had once thumbed through when he was young. His readers hadn't been bothered, and shortly after its publication a grateful manufacturer of sporting bows had told him how it had increased worldwide demand for his products.

He leaned down—the chair emitted a groan and he felt a brief twinge in his back—and took the ammunition clips out of the drawer. With careful hands, eyes narrowed and lips pursed, he loaded the pistol, pushing a clip into the magazine, then pulling back the bolt, and letting it snap forward again—something you see so often in films that he realized it made him feel unintentionally like an actor when he did it himself.

The sun had set, flames of red dissolved themselves in the water, the mountain peaks glinted with an icy light, and between the hovels of the favelas he could see the snaking lines of unpaved streets. Miguel Auristos Blanco stood up, reached for the four letters his secretary had selected from the day's mail (every day he received innumerable pleas for advice and help, along with tearful life stories, offers of marriage, prayers, and manuscripts of novels which were about either the search for life's meaning or UFOs, plus invitations to conferences in dozens of cities, where there were directors of libraries, meditation centers, and bookshops who knew that this man was so busy he had no time to make personal appearances but didn't want to give up hope that he would make an exception for them just this once, and extracted the first out of its envelope, which had already been slit open for him.

It was written on handmade deckled paper, with the letterheading of the United Nations, under which was the inquiry as to whether, if the jury decided in his favor, he would accept the Dialogue Between the Nations Award and be prepared to address the General Assembly. He smiled. The second letter was from his biographer Camier in Lyons asking in his respectful tiny handwriting for a further interview to discuss his time in a Japanese monastery thirty years ago, his study of the koans, the wisdom of the East, and of course his first, second, and third marriages; as always, Camier assured him, he could rely on the discretion of the authorized biographer that nothing that he didn't want would end up in print. Miguel Auristos Blanco paused. He didn't believe Camier, but what could he do other than agree to the interview?

The third in the stack, without an envelope, was a postcard from Tenerife, where Aurelia was now living with their two children. The house, formerly belonging to both of them, was now hers exclusively, and it was almost a year since the last time he'd seen Luis and Laura. He had wondered all that time why he didn't miss them more, and to explain it to himself, he had added a whole chapter to *Ask the Cosmos, It Will Speak* about how we only suffer the absence of those whose souls are not in harmony with our own. Whereas those closest to us who are part, as it were, of our very being, arouse no need in us to have them at our side, for what they feel, we feel, regardless of how far away they are, and what they suffer, we suffer, and every actual conversation with them is no more than a superfluous confirmation of the self-evident. He spent thirty seconds contemplating the photograph on the front (bay, mountains, flag, swarm of seagulls) and the two little signatures, then he set the card aside.

The fourth letter was from Sra. Angela João, the abbess of the Carmelite Convent of the Holy Providence in Belo Horizonte, who asked him in the name of that old friendship (either his memory was failing or hers was, because he couldn't remember ever having met her) for some words on theodicy for her edification and that of her sister nuns: why did suffering exist, why did loneliness, why above all was God so utterly distant, and yet why was the world so perfectly organized?

He shook his head irritably. He would soon need a new secretary. This one was obviously suffering from overload. No letter as tiresome as this one should ever have reached his desk.

The boats were casting enormously long shadows, the water shimmered blood-red, and dark fire flared in the sky. He had watched countless sunsets from this window, yet every one of them seemed like the first to him, and he felt he was witnessing a complicated experiment that could go horribly wrong from one evening to the next. He put the letter down pensively and took the pistol, his fingers searching instinctively, as they had the last time, three days ago, for the safety catch, until he realized that Glocks don't have one and that on this particular model the trigger itself was the safety catch. He pointed the weapon at himself and looked into the mouth of the barrel. He'd often done it before, of an evening, usually around about this time, and as always he could feel himself begin to sweat. He put the pistol down, switched on the computer, and waited for the machine to laboriously boot up. Then he began to write.

But why? He himself didn't really know. Perhaps it was mere politeness, because a question demanded an answer, perhaps also because old women in their religious habits had filled him all his life with a mixture of respect and absolute terror. Dear Abbess, venerable and blessed Reverend Mother, God cannot be justified, life is atrocious, its beauty amoral, even peace is filled with crimes, and no matter whether He exists or not—I've never made up my mind about that—I have no doubt that my miserable death will evoke no more pity in Him than the deaths of my children or, some day may it be long distant, Reverend Mothers, yours.

He hesitated, blinked into the last fiery rays of the sun, tilted his head back, and took a deep breath. He listened to the silence. The air conditioning was humming quietly. Then he went back to writing.

He wrote while the sun was sending its last glow across the water; he wrote while the air slowly filled with darkness as if with some fine substance; he wrote while the lights down there glittered more and more distinctly and the smooth black expanse of the sky blended into the mountains; and when he looked up, his shirt wet and his moustache covered with drops of sweat, it was night. Dear Abbess, there are no grounds for hope, and even if God's existence were to be justified by something other than His flagrant absence, every intelligent argument would still pale before the scale of suffering in the world, before the very fact that suffering exists, and that everything always and eternally, think about this, Reverend Mother, is stained with imperfection. The only things that help us are consoling lies such as the dignity incarnated in your sainted person. May you remain in this state for many years and in fond memory I remain yours, etc. . . . He double-clicked on the mouse and the printer began to hum. A sheet, another sheet, a third, and then a fourth filled up with letters. Miguel Auristos Blanco picked up the tiny pile and began read.

He got to his feet. How had he written this? These pages were the absolute retraction of everything, the annihilation of his life's work, the clear, concise apology for his ever having claimed that there was an order in the world and life could be good.

But it wasn't until he reached a tanned hand out for the pistol that he understood what he'd done, and that the time when he'd thought he still had a choice was over. What had been a quasi-game before was suddenly real. If he really did squeeze the trigger, he would make history. All the world's believers, all the optimists, and the prayerful who had his books in their bookcases and his example in their hearts— how could he resist the temptation to deliver such a blow to them! This, and only this, would make him a great man. The corners of his mouth twitched in a mixture of laughter and panic. What he had just written wasn't even his own opinion. It was simply the truth.

His knees were suddenly weak; he leaned against the window. The winking lights of a plane drew a curve in the firmament, a boat fired off a flare that soared and burst silently in a whirl of sparks. In the room next door, with a poor sense of timing, the cleaning lady turned on the vacuum cleaner.

He picked up the last sheet one more time and asked himself if he really had written it, and how after so many years of being emollient he could have come up with these words. He had a vision of the Church congresses and their tables of books from which his would be banished, he had a vision of bookshops with gaps in their shelves, he had a vision of shocked priests and blanching housewives, bewildered doctors' wives and all the middle-ranking employees on five continents, to whom there would be no one left to say that their suffering had meaning. He dropped the piece of paper, and before it could float to the floor on the draft from the air conditioner that carried it gently this way and that, he picked up the pistol. No safety catch. You only had to pull the trigger. He opened his mouth and clenched his teeth around the polymer barrel, which to his surprise wasn't even cold.

His fingers groped for the trigger. Eyes wide, as the sweat ran down over his forehead, he saw the city below, the twinkling lights of the boats, the expanse of the night. The bullet would pass through his head and hit the window—as if to strike not just the glass but the universe itself, as if the cracks would run through the sea, the mountains, and the sky, and he grasped that this was the truth, that this was exactly what would happen if he and only he branded the world with the sigh of his contempt, once and for all, if only he had the strength to pull the trigger. He heard himself panting. In the room next door the vacuum cleaner droned. If.

A Contribution to the Debate

ere I have to back up. Sorry: perfectly clear that lithuania23 and icu_lop will flame this posting for being too long; so will that troll lordoftheFlakes, just like he flamed on MovieForum, but I can't do it shorter, and whoever's in a hurry can just skip it. Meeting celebrities? Heads up!

Must signal that I'm a huge hardcore fan of this forum. Platinum idea. Normal types like you and me who spot famous people and report on their sightings: chill, no? wicked idea, really well worked out, interesting to everyone and besides it acts like control, so they know they're being scanned and can't just goof off. Wanted to post here forever, only where to get the stuff. But then came last weekend, the whole load.

Quick flashback. (My life has been the whole crazy load recently, but you have to cope, there are good days and bad days, yin and yang stuff and for you freaks who've never heard of that: it's philosophy!) You know my username moll-wit from other forums. I post a lot on Supermovies and also on TheeveningNews, on literature4you, and chat rooms, and when I see bloggers serving up bullshit I let them have it. Username always mollwit. In Real Life (the real one!) I'm in my mid-thirties, quite tall, medium build. During the week I wear tie, office regs, whole capitalist racket, you do the same. Has to happen if you're going to realize your Life Sense. In my case writing analyses, observations, and debates: contributions to culture, society, political stuff.

I work in the headquarters of a cell phone company and share an office with Lobenmeier, whom I hate, the way nobody's ever hated anybody, you can eat lunch on that. I wish him dead, and if there's worse than dead then I wish him that too. Logicalwise he's the boss's golden boy, day-on-day punctual, yes yes yes hardworking, and for as long as he's at his desk, he does his work stuff and only stops to look at me and say something like "hey, back on the Internet again?" Sometimes he jumps up, comes round my desk, and wants to eyeball my screen, but I'm quicker and click off in time. Just the once I had to go to the water closet in a hurry and I left a couple windows open by accident, and when back, he was sitting on my chair with a huge smiley face. I swear to you, if he wasn't a fitness freak, he'd have swallowed his teeth right then.

Our boss seriously awful too. Totally unchill and majorly bad, none of your small stuff. I think he trusts me, but you can't tell with him: he's always thinking us through and hatching plans nobody can overview. Power plays totally above my head; for me, it's about the universal thing and society and all the daily pig stuff . . . you know. Obvious that people who write for newspapers already bought, and people they write about in it with them. A huge conspiracy, everyone in bed together, coining money like mad, us okay people just waiting. Just one example: radio messages on 9/11, read it online, nothing will surprise you again!

Back to topic. All began last Friday. Was about to post on movieforum of TheeveningNews, about Ralf Tanner and the slap. Bugclap4 said nothing going on any more with him and Carla Mirelli, while icu_lop thought still something to be saved. I was one who knew more again, had read something on another Web site, but when I wanted to go public, noticed I couldn't post any more. Wouldn't work! Whole load of error messages each time, and because it stank I just called up.

Okay, okay, okay, okay, clear already. Didn't think. I know. But evening before to top everything banged heads with mother again: you can cook for yourself, you can wash your own stuff, like that plus more, finally me back "So live alone, pay your own rent!"

Then her: "Never wanted to move here! And you'd really rather be with some *tramp*!"

Then me: "go back to flyspeckland, cow!"

Around midnight, kiss-up scene in cinemascope, but next day I was still cross-wired and all down-side up, otherwise none of it would have happened.

So, looked up number, dialed. So furious, could hear heart thump-beating.

Voice answering man. Me: "my postings aren't being posted! Already the fourth time."

Voice: How, what, postings where? No explanations there.

Me: explanations, explanations, blablah, then him "connecting you now!"

Then second and third technotype, and that's exactly when Lobenmeier came back and smiled like a moosehead while the technotype asked for name and location and IP address and Ethernet ID. Then typed, yawned, typed, stopped. "Give me the IP again."

Me: "Problems?"

He typed, stopped, typed, then asked if it's possible I've already posted twelvethousandthreeehundredfortyone times on TheeveningNews.

"And?"

Him again: "twelvethousandthreeehundredfortyone!"

"So?"

Him, third time. This not going anywhere. I hung up.

I know you're uproaring with laughter. But no one is a hundred percent on alert, and shit occurs. When I tried again, the posting went through at once, and there was so much to do that I didn't give it another thought. Discussion already far along, high time for someone to bring voice of reason. Ralf Tanner and Carla Mirelli, I wrote, it will never be anything again, he has sawdust in his head and is as ugly as an ox, you can forget it!

Only hours later did I begin to suspect I had done a really dumb thing. Real names, real addresses, the IP. I was now a whole load visible. Very bad feeling, and for real. Was chain-ganging again and no way to brainwave: major fight going on with lonebulldoggy on Thetree.com and at the same time I had to check through some Achtung from the technical department about mess-ups in the phone number bank that the boss had slapped on my desk. I'd had it for two days. Had forwarded it to Hauberlan, who obviously felt he had to send it on upstairs, probably just to darken me, the Überswine is in league with Lobenmeier. And suddenly the boss calls.

Result: general brown-trouser alert and whole load of heartrace. Of course thought: must be the IP thing already. Stand up, go, tell myself to stay cool as a fridge. I'm not a No-gump, have already written things in the German Chancellor's online Guestbook but they got all erased no one can just flatten me like that, I can dish it out to anyone when I have to.

So am standing in front of the boss, and he's looking at me. Piercingly. Like Saruman. Or Vorlone-Kosh from *Babylon 5*. Looking at me and me looking back. Fridgeorama. Two men, one look. Giant screen encounter.

Blahblahing about Congress of European Telecommunications Providers, Startgo day after tomorrow. Wanted to go himself, couldn't. Department had to be represented, also presentation made: National versus European frequency norms.

Took me some time to figure out. Oh fuckingshit. What? You have to know I hate the travel thing a whole load. The seats in the trains are crazy narrow so that normal human person can't get backside into them. And a presentation in front of strangers, I don't think so.

Me in sequence: no, and won't work, and have other plans, but him: nonsense, you have to, you're the best. So what to say? Me: "Okay boss!" And him: "You're my man!" and me: "no, no stop!" and him: "but it's true!" and so on back and forth and back again, then me back in my office.

On the way home to tranquilize, the new book by Miguel Auristos Blanco. Writes that you shouldn't take things to heart: *learn to accept.* Bingo! *Which is better, to cover the earth with a carpet or to put on shoes?* Must write that down. Wow. Where does someone like that find that stuff?

Then more row with mother. Away whole weekend, oh really, and how would she spend her time, and if I don't care.

Me: "So go out. Go to a movie!"

"Don't know, don't want to! And don't believe you, you're meeting a tramp."

Me: "Rubbish, nothing there" and so on.

Her: "Don't pretend. You're meeting one. And me alone at home. If only I'd known that thirty-seven years ago, you were such a darling, so little."

Me: "So move out if it doesn't suit you!" What I always say to her, now you know.

"And who will cook for you?"

Okay. Point for her. So leave her standing, slam the door, lock myself in. Leaf through Auristos Blanco and try parallel move to get into Moviechat with DotB. No chance of course, server overloaded, everyone trying, logical outcome. *Become one with things, one with becoming one, one with your oneness with them, one with your anger too, and if the atom bomb should fall, then become one with the bomb.* Big Bang Theory. I know, I'm too busy, too much work, too much day-in-day-out, but the super-thoughts, recognize those asap, soon as I see them. Then distracted by lordoftheflakes, usual bullshit, and by proctor, zheligoland, and pearfriend who've got hits on his site, and two new posters I don't know at all and have to bellyslash right there. (Could also be that lordoftheflakes had new Nicks. Sort of thing drives me nuts, disgusting. Have three other names, me too of course, but only use them when baddest bad guys leave me no choice.) Transparent that I ought to have prepared my presentation, but it wasn't until the day after tomorrow and I couldn't concentrate right now. Shortly before midnight, a couple more private sites. Sweet, if you understand one, none of those brutal ones, they're not for me and then went to bed.

Next day: train trip. Felt sick, seats too narrow—surprise—but not full-full so I could lift armrest and spread over two. Out there little house, roads, meadowswamp things, the whole view-from-the-train bit. Then exit, escalator down, escalator up, hard to breathe, sweating like a pig. But made my connection, more meadowswamps, farmhouses, fields of mustard. Six hours, already crazy-nervous could barely remember last time offline for so long. Finally arrive, driver with minibus to collect me and other Congress types. All ties and briefcases, the usual.

"Traveling: hell," I said to the neighboring nerd along the way. "And for what! We could do everything from home by V.IP! I'd see you, you'd see me, everything easy-peasy, no stress." But the nerd just stared and then slid away along the seat.

At Reception, I demanded instant Internet. The woman looked at me like an obelisk. "Internet! Hello, Internet!"

Her: "not working right now."

"Pardon, what, how, huh?"

Her: yes, so sorry, service interrupted at the moment, usually the rooms have wi-fi, but not for now.

Me: just stared. Couldn't get it.

"It'll be fixed next week."

Me: Fanbloodytastic. Really helps me. What's the prob?

Stared at me blank. Sarcasm: new territory for her. So shocked felt faint. Hotel parked in booniest boondocks. No village, no Internet café, so either someone lent me his HSDPA card, or situation pitch-black. And come on, nobody lends you their Internet card, everyone's afraid you'll download movies at company expense. So: catastrophe. Catacombs. Night night.

Dinner. No need to describe it to you, you know it: food-fight at buffet, pushing, shoving. Everything good already gone when you want some. Then at table: to my right, a bearded type from T-Mobile talking about his new wooden floor, to my left a female skeleton from Vodaphone has a cousin of her brother-in-law's who's scored an Opel at rock-bottom price. Me: radio silence. Never say anything in front of strangers. Can't, won't, no app. Went back to buffet instead, then again, then I would toss, then out into parking lot, nicotine fix. Not allowed to smoke inside, not allowed to smoke anywhere. Telling you, no worse under the Nazis.

Rain, a whole load. Under porch roof, man with a cigarette. Almost dark by now, so at first only saw his outline and luminous red dot. Asked for a light, and while he groped nervously, recognized him.

"Leo Richter!"

Jumped. Looked at me. It was him!

Okay. So I'm asking you: What would you have done? Pre-amble: been a fan of his for years, totally crazy. That one book, don't remember title, Lara Gaspard teaching in Paris meets these totally wasted types and then in the last story goes down to the Underworld. Read it, totally crazy, couldn't believe it, mega-trip. The style, the wit, smokin' good, but most of all, the woman. Have to add have never been winner with opposite sex, all that roundabout stuff and blablah and then always "Leave me alone, you're a nice guy but not that way, now go!" and so on, all the bullshit you guys know, and on FindyourLove, even if it was all A-1 to begin with, the moment I put my photo online, blackout. Contact gone? But Lara, for sure, wouldn't have happened that way with her. She's not superficial. And though she looks crazy-good, she's also so smart she doesn't care about a man's outsides. And she thinks like me! And me like her. Know you're not supposed to read books that way, but sometimes . . . well, seem crazy to you?

I mean, I know she's a made-up person. And that—of course I googled as soon as I'd read it—Leo Richter wrote it when he was in Paris himself and then when his wife gave him the boot came the three stories where Lara leaves her husband, *The Moon and Freedom, Herr Müller and Eternity,* forget the title of the third. So, the shit that happens to him then happens to her, what he does, she does later, and whoever meets him can surface in story. In the Literaturehouse chat room, somebody called this *autobiographical narcissism,* but I flamed him and he won't ever chat again about stuff he doesn't get, dumpster dog. Only story I didn't like was the one about the old lady going to Switzerland to throw the poison down, he wasn't in it anywhere, and the ending made no sense, no idea who could see through it, not me for sure.

"Your book! Where d'you think I read it?"

Hiccups. Logical: the excitement. Hard to talk to strangers, don't normally do it. But I was crazy-excited. "Between Munich and Brussels! Dining car! Finished it as we pulled into the station."

He looked at me. Turned away, then back to me. Strange moves, sort of angular and nervous.

"Exactly the right length! You leave Munich, you start. You reach Brussels, you're done. Wicked! I was going to a seminar on UMTS."

"Remarkable," he said.

(Hey, not making this up. Wrote his words down as soon as I got to my room. Why? Logical—for this forum.)

Me: Where do you get your ideas?

He turned away, looked down at the gravel, then up at the porch roof. "In the bathtub."

"Really? Chill! Fact?"

"Promise."

"Chiller than chill. Eat my socks! Bathtub."

Then both of us silent for a time. He smoked, I smoked, the rain did its raining thing.

Then me: "And are you writing right now? What's Lara doing, what's in the plan? Can I stop being formal with you?"

He threw his cigarette away. "I have to go back in."

"What are you doing here? Of all the gin joints?"

"Lecture."

"Hey?"

"A bank's giving a seminar and they contacted my agent to book me. I thought why not, a few days in the green. But it doesn't ever stop raining." Looked at me, as if it was my fault, and again, "Ever!" Turned around and back into the house. Me: Stood there, smoked one more, chilled, and tried to figure out what had just gone on. My God. Wow. Then went up to my room.

I admit, my head was cross-wired and scramble-brained. Too much colliding: the fight with mother and being so stupid as to give out my IP. And worry about tomorrow: okay, a pro like me can make a presentation, but I hadn't netsurfed for nine and a half hours, no longer up to speed with anything! Not a spark about how lordoftheflakes, icu_lop, ruebendaddy, and pray4us had responded to my postings. Made my stomach heave just to think of it. Potatoed in front of the TV, but nothing but world-level shit, and then I see there was no shower, only a tub, so narrow you couldn't fit in it. So today would be hygienically challenged too.

A few minutes on the laptop. PowerPoint, not easy to use. Typed a little, moved some windows around, couldn't get it to work. Well, it would have to work tomorrow morning. So bed, lights out, clutch pillow. The dream Olympics, as mother always says.

But couldn't sleep. One floor down, sounds of whole choir of drunken nerds. Constant thundering of feet in the corridor. Always like that with Congresses, the desk jockeys can't handle it and down the booze like drains. Funny ideas in my head. Holy Ninjas: being in the same house as Leo Richter, who made up Lara Gaspard. The guy who decided what she saw and did. Shaking his hand was almost like shaking hers—you pierce my meaning?

And then, at that moment, in the darkness of my room, I had an A-1 flash. If you're surfing the net as much as I am, then you know—how to say it? Well, you know that reality isn't everything. That there are spaces you don't enter with your body. Only in your thoughts, but definitely there. Meeting Lara Gaspard. *It was possible!* In a story, of course.

Leo used stuff he saw? Guys he met? Events that happened? Yes, he could even use me. Nothing against it! Appearing in a story—really no different from being in a chat room. Transformation! Transport yourself into some other place. In a story I'd be someone else, but also me. In the same world as Lara.

You on my page? I crazy-worship this man, and I wanted to get into a story. He had to get to know me. I had to make him notice me! Either become his buddy or—main thing, had to notice me! My whole shit life, the nonstop fights with

Mama, my dog boss, and that huge porker Lobenmeier: I felt suddenly there was a deliverance. As I went to sleep, I was happier than I'd been for long time. And you know what else? I felt light.

Next morning: wake-up. Still no luck with the bathtub, far too narrow. Went down to breakfast room. Made mistake of three plates, one in the left hand, one in the right, and one balanced in the middle, and of course preciselyexactly that one fell: scrambled eggs on the floor, bacon stuff, two rolls, everything garbage fodder. Leo was sitting far back against the wall, alone. Approached him, naturally, and "Slept well, hombre?"

He stared. Funny way of watching. Eyes wide, mouth twitching nonstop. Relaxed, believe me, he's not.

"Didn't get the chance to talk yesterday!" Began to eat. Blob of scrambled egg fell down, paid no attention. "Do you want to know something about me?"

"Pardon?"

Said my name and where I work and gave him a brief outline of what my department in the company preciselyexactly does. Also said something about my mother and what it's like to share your office with a pig.

"Have to go," he said.

"Your breakfast? You didn't finish yet!"

Already gone: exit, door, out. Nervous guy, writer, what d'you want. Ate the two pieces of toast he'd smeared with marmalade, would have been a waste, then went to Reception and demanded Internet. What d'you think? Dungheap. Catacombs. And then: Conference room.

Don't worry, not going to rigidify you with the details. A conference, right. Flipcharts, tables, lots of handshakes around the place, but none with me. Just one guy wanting to know about our department but what are you supposed to say? Looked at him silently till he went away. Then finally lunch break: rolled ham, mayo, eggs, quiche, it went, have had worse. Coming back with my third plate, okay, it was admittedly a little bit full up, a guy got in my way, and "Are you taking precautionary measures against a crisis?" Me, rocketing right back: "Fuck you, pigshit filthsow die!" And he just vanished. Sometimes just flip my lid. Not good, I know, regret it afterward, but can't help it.

A few minutes left in the break. So back to Reception. "Need to have quick conversation with Leo Richter, please."

She typed on her keyboard, then picked up the receiver, Leo on the line. Must have been asleep. "Who?"

Give my name again.

"Who?"

Unbelievable. He'd forgotten me again already. "Thought we'd grab a bite together? Lots to tell you. Unbelievable stories, you can really use them. I've had quite a life."

But then, a sharp noise and a click, connection interrupted. Crap hotel. Immediately dialed again. "Me again, so what about lunch?"

He coughed. Sounded influenza'd to the max. "Can't."

"Later?"

Silence.

"You still there?"

Silence.

"You coming to my presentation?"

"Difficult. I've got a lot . . ."

"European versus national frequency norms. Interesting for you too!"

He cleared his throat.

"Look, a phone uses something called ISM Codes, for identification purposes. Example: You want to issue an order and you're not on your home network. If you—"

Click and the engaged signal. That was no accident, I'm not brain-dead, he hung up on me! Artists: shy, you have no idea.

And me: heart-bangingly nervous, and how. Crystal-clear, logicwise of course: the presentation. Right after the break, so now, no exit, no time, close my eyes and go.

Everyone already in the room. Someone gave me hand, then another, than another, didn't know any of them, and up front at the microphone some type in tie announcing unfortunately my boss not here, but me in his place, then applause. Me, up on platform. Three steps, quite steep, once up there, totally out of breath and sweating. Open laptop, plug in network cable, my PowerPoint started right up on the screen, the technical stuff really A-1 here, you'd have liked it, and off we went, the complete enchilada.

To begin with, it was aces. Everything clear, the flipcharts flipped, and I talked New Approach and the national security protocols for UMTS, pros and cons, glitches and possibilities, everything clockwork. Then I see Leo.

Or maybe not. You know, darkened room, two spotlights

on my face, and no chance to see if the Darth Vader–black shape right at the back was him or not. My invitation, after all. His size, the nervous twitching were right, and he kept rubbing his head. But his face? I leaned forward, useless, saw nothing. From then on, it was curtains for me.

Stuttered. And how. The whole nine yards. Words disappeared in the middle of sentences, then the laptop went on the fritz and blocked the graphics. And my hand so wet, couldn't work the mouse. Felt everyone looking at me, burning. Wouldn't wish it on any of you (no, not true: lordoftheflakes). And then a thought: Leo could really use this! A good guy, knows his stuff, but goes to pieces big-time during lecture. Chill story? You can bet on it. And suddenly was seeing myself from the outside as if it wasn't me; result more stuttering, and result more stuttering still.

Hands sweating even more, mouse fell down, clattered on the floor, and bending over impossible, what to do? Stood there gaping, clueless. Then somebody out there in the middle laughed. Then somebody else at the back. Then three women in the first row, then everybody. Asked myself if I was dreaming. Had had dreams like that, so have you, so has everyone. But this was for real, one to one, Life Reality, the full program. Managed another few sentences, then thought flash: "What if that's it?" And that's what happened, I heard myself not hearing myself any longer because my voice was gone and I saw myself standing there looking at myself standing there looking at myself. Hell. And meantime they were laughing. I still managed to get it together to say into the microphone that I wasn't feeling well, then that I was faintingfitsick, gross-out, then back down the three steps, luckily without landing flat. A tie-guy asked if I needed doctor, but I told him to mind his own business, and out of there.

Absolutely flatass. Sweating like a sauna. Dizzy, boneless. Every part soaked. Had to cool down somehow, come down, be chill again. Looked around lobby. And right then I spotted guy getting up from table, direction restroom, laptop abandoned—and it had a WiFi stick! Snuck up closer. And closer. Then down into the chair, typed furiously, foot on the gas. First stop Movieforum, and yes, in response to my totally factual posting, bugclap had flamed me so fiercely it took my breath away—what is it with you guys, don't you have a life? Replied express, had to.

Flashback the lecture again. When shit finds fan, flies in bucketloads. Hands trembling: Quick into chat room, where I told pray4us what needed telling since forever, dumb as pigshit, die. Then into my mailbox. No messages—thought again about having given out my IP. Was someone already after me? Because the bigshots are ruthless. They do whatever they want, and I'd insulted everyone from the President on down. Then went into TheeveningNews and said today's lead article was all bullshit. Hadn't read a word of it, but so what, they'd take it down anyway, and it helped, feeling calmer already. At that moment, from beside me "Hey what's going on?"

Me: huh, what, what d'you? I'd already forgotten. Head pretty cross-wired, believe me.

"You, that's my computer!"

What big retort is there in a case like that? So me: Apologies, sorry, error, the whole shitload. Stood up, went through the lobby. Just then, saw people coming out of one of the other conference rooms: tie-guys and women in silk stuff, but in the middle: guess who!

I was speed itself. Heard someone say, "Do you know where I read it? In the plane from Hamburg to Madrid." Leo nodded. He looked peculiar.

Another one: "Where do you get your ideas?"

Leo twitched, turned around, swayed a little. The whole nervousness deal. "Have to go work now!"

"What a won-der-ful lecture!" A woman. Glasses, a real wrinklie, upswept hair. "You have made us think!"

And another: "You'll stay to have dinner with us?"

In your dreams. I manipulate his shoulder and "Out of discussion, we have an appointment!" Stressissime for me, crazy to madness, sweating saunas, but didn't let it show. "No boringness, we're going for a drink Misterman Leo the Writer, we're off."

But he pulled himself away and ran to Reception and "Room 305, key." I can tell you this exactly because I heard it with fine ears and know the vitalness of exactitude online and precise info and datastuff as soon as you have something. Have thought about it often since, but supercertain, no doubt, 305, I heard it!

Then Leo to the elevator, so fast I couldn't follow him: I'm not so lightfoot. Next to me, the woman says to the tie-guys

"What a pity. It was really mah-vell-ous." To which one of them "Okay, but he really isn't very appealing." And the third: "I thought it was so-so." And the woman again, to me "And who are you?"

Didn't want to talk to them. So button lip and leave, head for bar, order whisky. Then another. Charged to the company of course. And another. Tie-types went by, turned their heads toward me, laughed. You know, those people who at a certain point grab a gun-thing and then it's blood by the square yard, I can understand them. It's just I'm not that type. I don't know artillery, wouldn't know where to get it, unfortunately.

One whisky doesn't do much for me, I need several before I feel anything. After the fourth however, downhill slalom. Vertigo, thick tongue, eyes frozen, the whole effectsofalcohol program, you know it all, don't have to explain. But suddenly I was so sad. And didn't know what to do anymore.

Lara Gaspard. Now or never. So I got up (ethylo-alcoholic impediments notwithstanding), took elevator to the third floor. 305.

Knocked. Nothing.

Knocked louder.

Nothing.

Banged with fist.

Chambermaid suddenly next to me. Of course total panic and sorry and my mistake and started to go when she: "Did you lock yourself out?"

And me right away: "Exactly!" Because when in need, I

can cogitate like lightning, Spock's a koala compared to me. So she does the card thing into the slit, beep, door opens, I'm in. Switched on the light. Everything empty, bed untouched, no Leo.

Sweat event. I had thought that was over, but you know what? With sweat, there's always more. Leo Richter's room, I thought. Looked around, opened drawers, cupboards—Lara Gaspard's room. Somehow hers as well. My God.

Usual stuff in the cupboards. Underwear, a laptop (booted it up, but required password), couple of books: Plato, Hegel, Bhagavad Gita. Unnecessary, the lot of them, it's all in *What the Thinkers Tell Us* by Auristos Blanco, only much clearer and easier to pierce. I squatted on the bed. Listen, no bullshit, I was completely at fours and fives. And afraid of course: if Leo came in now he'd be perfectly capable of calling for help. But I had to reach his awareness somehow. Had to get into the story. Because what else did I have? It was a one-time opportunity. I'd have hit him in the chops if that would have helped, but he wasn't there.

As I looked around, the room looked—well, don't ask. Craziness: drawers pulled out, papers strewn around, computer on the floor, screen probably busted. Sheets torn out of the notepad and all crumpled up. Bedcover on the carpet, in the bathroom, everything dropped onto the tiles, glass splinters. Was that me? I couldn't tell you. Then I lay in his bed for a bit. So soft. Cried for a long time into the pillow. Thought about Lara.

Then out again, quick. Along the corridor to the elevator,

down to my room. Just made it to bed. Legs collapsed, lay there, and the ceiling was spinning abovebelowabovebelow me, everything mixed up with everything else, my God was I drunk.

I woke up to pounding head. Everything soaked, banging behind my forehead and taste in my mouth as if some animal had died in there. Seven a.m. Seven messages on the phone from mother. Had slept in my clothes again. Two clicks and it all came back to me.

I had to talk to him. That was it: talk to him, admit everything exactly the way it happened, the way I've just told you now. Didn't matter what he did next, he wouldn't be able to resist it, because it was a real story. My entry into fiction. Right now, at breakfast.

So took myself to breakfast room and waited. Ate toast, ate muesli, ate scrambled eggs. Drank coffee. Leafed through two newspapers. Not familiar with TheeveningNews in print version, only online, interesting, there was a tech-page that wasn't half bad, but it only reminded me that I couldn't get online, so I quickly set it aside. Ate some rolls, two sausages, some salmon, chunk of salami, two pieces of toast with marmalade, more scrambled eggs. Mother never makes a decent breakfast. Always says "make it yourself, buy your own stuff if you don't like mine!" and so on. So nervous. He'd be here any minute.

But he didn't come. Only nerds from yesterday who looked at me and grinned and whispered. I swear to you: if I weren't such a peaceable person, then it would be pumpguns, hell, shots to the head, inferno, the whole load.

Finally went out into the hall. The woman behind the Reception desk was already shaking her head: "no, no, no Internet yet."

"Want to speak to Leo Richter!"

"He's no longer here."

"What?"

"Left last night."

Okay, so I got a little loud. I shouldn't have banged on the table, at least not with both fists. But I shouldn't have asked her whose room I'd just totally zeroed. Luckily her understanding pierced nothing and I clammed asap, I do not have a brain of mush. Then I abandoned the field and called mother.

All alone, she said. Had cried all day. "Are you going to keep doing this? Do you have a tramp?"

None, I promised her. Anywhere!

"Don't believe you!"

I began to cry too. I know it sounds crazy-pitiful. But I'm telling you because you don't know me and you don't know who I am. Right there in the lobby.

Okay, she said, it's all right. "I do believe you. But promise you won't ever do it again. The whole weekend. Alone in the house. Never again, okay?"

I promised.

So okay, why not? I had no problem with it. Would anyone else ever want to spend time with me? At least I now had some stuff for the SpottheStars forum. But I can see already that it has no punch line, no hooks, nothing. No basis for a story.

For I'll never see Leo again. I did a posting on literaturehouse.com that his books are all shit, did it on Amazon too, bigtime. But this changes nothing. He'll never read that stuff.

The hotel guys didn't want to give me a thing, no address, no phone number. He won't write anything about me, I'll never meet Lara. Reality will be the only thing I have: job and mother at home and the boss and the Überpig Lobenmeier, and the only escape forums like this. (At least I'm no troll like lordoftheflakes, or a brainless custard like icu_lop or pray4us.) All I have forever is me. Only right here, on this side. I'll never get onto the other side, never. No alternative universe. Early tomorrow, back to work. Weather forecast terrible. Even if it were good, so what? Everything goes on the way it always has. And I know now that I'll never, ever, be in a story.

How I Lied and Died

I met Luzia one Wednesday evening at a reception in the Bureau of Regulation of Telecommunications Licenses, and from that day on I became a liar and I was lost.

I had been together with Hannah for nine years—in principle at least, for she lived with our son and our baby daughter, a somewhat strange infant, in a peaceful dull town on a lake in southern Germany where I had been born and now spent the weekends. The workweeks, however, I spent alone in a gray suburb of Hannover which the enterprise that employed me had chosen as its headquarters. Hannah was a little older than I was and she was comfortable being on her own. I wasn't that important to her anymore—she knew it, and I knew it too, and each of us knew that the other one knew. But she was Hannah, we had a noisily suckling baby at home, and it was clear to me immediately that Luzia must remain unaware of this.

I'll describe her later, when the moment comes. Here, let

me just say that she was tall, with dark blond hair, and her eyes were brown and round like a hamster's: brilliant, never focusing on anything for more than a few seconds, a little anxious. I noticed her when she dropped her glass on the floor and then immediately broke a vase of flowers that someone had foolishly left standing around on a pedestal. She was wearing a sleeveless dress, the skin on her upper arms was flawless, and as I saw her standing over the debris, I knew I would rather die than renounce the chance to hold her in my arms, mingle my breath with hers, and watch her eyes right up close as they rolled back under their lids.

She was a chemist. I didn't understand what she did; it involved carbon and the synthesis of something, and even tangentially with nuclear fusion and the production of energy out of nothing. I nodded a lot, said Aha, yes, of course, and bent over to smell her perfume. When she asked what I did and what had brought me here—I didn't know if she meant the city or this reception—I had to think before I was able to answer her: the circumstances of my life now seemed as foreign and as far away as the weather on the other side of the planet.

I was—at that time at least, because I'm unemployed today, and the likelihood of being hired by another company is not large—the head of the department of the administration and assignment of phone numbers in one of the large telecommunications companies. It may sound boring, but in reality it's even more boring than that. It wasn't what was forecast over my cradle, and it wasn't what my mother expected when she talked about her son's brilliant future. I once played the piano well, I could paint adequately, and all the photos of me show a pretty child with intelligent eyes. But the world breaks almost all of us, and why should my particular dreams have come true, reading books isn't a profession, my father said, and angry as I was at the time, when my children reach that age I'll tell them the same thing: reading books isn't a profession. So I studied applied electronics with an emphasis on mobile communications, learned about the then-still-standard analog mobile phones (it seems an eternity ago), about SID and MIN codes, and all the methods for sending a human voice around the world in millionths of a second, started work, and gradually got used to sluggish afternoons in the office with the pervasive smell of coffee and ozone. At first I supervised five people, then seven, then nine, discovered to my amazement that people cannot work together without hating one another, and if you tell them what to do they detest you, met Hannah, whom I loved more than she loved me, became head of a department, and then was moved to another town; it's called a career. I was being paid well, I was very lonely, and in the evenings I read books in Latin with the help of a dictionary or watched TV sitcoms with laugh tracks and accepted that life is what it is, and that there were a few choices you could make yourself, but not many.

And now I was standing in front of Luzia, my heart was racing quite ridiculously, and I heard myself like a detective asking more and more systematic questions to find out whether she had a family or if there was someone in her life, in other words if there was any chance that someday or better quite soon or even better this evening I could put my lips on the little hollow above her clavicle. She laughed now and then, lifted and lowered her glass, and I saw her long neck and the play of muscles under the skin of her shoulders and the play of light on her silky hair, and all the while shadowy figures moved at the edge of my field of vision. Glasses clinked, people laughed, sentences were exchanged, and somewhere someone was giving a speech, but none of it interested me. She had only, said Luzia, arrived here recently, and, well, to tell the truth she didn't really like it; she laughed softly and I wasn't sure whether she'd really given me a flirtatious look or whether it was merely an illusion conjured up by the poor lighting and my desire.

"Do you have a phone?"

"Yes," I said, surprised. "Do you want to call someone?"

"No, it's ringing."

I reached into my pocket and pulled it out. The music I'd been hearing for awhile did indeed get louder. Hannah's name was on the screen. I hit the disconnect button. Luzia watched me, amused. I didn't understand why. I felt hot, and hoped I hadn't turned red.

"I've only had mine for a short time," she said. "I find it eerie. It makes everything unreal."

It took me a moment to understand that she was talking about her cell phone. I nodded and assured her she was absolutely right. I had no idea what she meant.

Only a few guests remained, glasses in hand, scattered around the room, and I wondered why she'd stayed this long, why in particular with me. I said we could go and find a drink elsewhere, the old well-worn formula, and she, as if she didn't understand or as if I didn't know she understood perfectly well, or as if she didn't know I knew, said yes, let's.

So we ended up in a rather uninviting bar, and Luzia talked, and I nodded, and now and again I said something too. The room seemed to be spinning slowly, I was incredibly conscious of her perfume, and when she touched my upper arm as if by accident, an electrical charge ran through my body, and when her hand brushed across my waist she didn't pull it back, and when at some point I came so close to her that I could see the tiny veins in the depth of her irises, I realized that I wasn't just living a wish or a dream anymore, or a fantasy born of my solitude, it was really happening.

"Do you live around here?" she asked.

At that moment my phone rang.

"Again?"

"A friend. He has a lot of problems. Calls at the oddest times: mornings, lunchtime, at night." I wasn't yet a practiced liar back then, and yet as I was saying it, I could see him in front of me in all his misery. Sad, drunk, unshaven, crushed by life, and desperate for my advice.

"Poor him," she said smiling. "Poor you."

"Yes," I said, in answer to her previous question. "Right around here."

It was actually quite far, the taxi took almost half an hour, and we sat side by side, embarrassed, like two strangers without a thing to say to each other. The driver smoked, oriental-sounding music was cooing out of the radio, and outside ragged-looking people were standing around under shop signs blinking meaninglessly into the night. It was cold, and the whole situation suddenly struck me as ridiculous. I remembered my bed wasn't made and I wondered how I was going to hide the plush elephant that had been in every bedroom I'd had since I was ten years old. The problem still seemed almost insoluble when we were in the stairwell. But then she didn't even notice it, and the unmade bed didn't matter either, nor the many dirty teacups lined up on the table, for we fell on each other before we were even through the door.

I was out of practice and when she pressed my back against the wall and her lips against my mouth, I couldn't breathe. Her hands were clamped around my neck, her knee pushed between my legs, beside me a book fell onto the floor, then she pulled me—I heard my shirt collar tear—into the middle of the room and shoved me so hard against the table that two of the empty cups were knocked off it. I threw my arms around her and held her tight against my body, partly out of desire and partly to prevent her from doing any more damage; for a few seconds that seem to me even now as being quite outside time, I saw her eyes a mere fraction of an inch from my own, and the smell of her surrounded me and our breath was a single breath. Perhaps this is the moment to pause and describe her.

She was half a head taller than me and had the broad shoulders of someone who grew up far from a city—quite different from my dark, fragile Hannah. Everything about her was massive; only her face was fine-featured, her brows delicately arched, her lips not too plump. Her breasts were larger and rounder than those of the distant woman I didn't want to think about right now. Was she beautiful? I couldn't have said, I still can't say, she was just herself, and for that reason I desired her so much that I would have given a year of my life, her life, anybody's life unhesitatingly for the privilege of touching her, and the moment when I actually did put my lips—she inhaled sharply—on her collarbone, my existence split into two halves: a before and an after, for all time.

An hour later we weren't even tired. Perhaps it was even longer, perhaps much less: time seemed to race forward and wind back, it folded itself into bows and tangles like unspooling film and afterward I no longer knew whether this was a result of my disordered memory or reality itself had succumbed to confusion. In one of my recollections I'm stretched out while her body lifts itself above me, silvery white in the dull light from the window, her hands on my shoulders, her head thrown back; in another she's lying under me, her hands digging into my back, her eyes turned away from me as my hand slides down her body to the place that makes her moan in despair or in pain. Or I in her arms or she in mine and the two of us half on the bed and half on the floor, so entwined that we could be one body or Siamese twins, her hand in my mouth and my arms around her hips—and at this precise moment Hannah's face flashes in front of me then fades again. Then we're on our feet and the back of my head bangs against the wall and I'm supporting her entire weight and the space around us disintegrates and then reassembles itself. Just at the moment when I succumb to gentle exhaustion, it all starts again and we clutch each other as if we were swimming in the Sargasso Sea because we don't want it to end. But finally we become separate, and there's her and there's me and I would love to have listened as she started telling me her life story but I'm already drifting into a dreamless sleep.

In the early morning it began again. Was I the one who shook her awake, or did she drag me from my sleep? I don't know, all I see is a clear, singularly pure sky in the window. Her hair on the white pillow had changed color in the dawn light and now was giving off red glints, but—she gave a sigh—we both sank back into sleep and the last dreams of the night that was ending.

When I woke up, she was fully dressed, murmured a goodbye, and was out the door; she had to get to work. I was late too. Without stopping for breakfast I ran to the car and while I was stuck as always in the 8 a.m. traffic, I called Hannah.

"Yesterday? Boring. The usual bunch of bureaucrats."

Even as I said it, I wondered about two things. First that people, even those closest to us who know us best, don't notice when we lie. The cliché holds the opposite, that you always betray yourself somehow and begin to stutter and sweat when you utter a falsehood, that you sound odd, that your voice changes. But friends, it's not true. And the fact that it's not true surprises nobody more than the liar. Besides, even if it were true, even if your voice tightened, even if we did sweat and blush and twitch, none of it would give us away because nobody notices. People are credulous, they don't anticipate being deceived. Who truly listens to other people, who concentrates on the chatter of his nearest and dearest? Everyone's mind is somewhere else.

"You poor thing. Those bores! I don't know how you stand it."

I detected no irony in her voice. And that was the other thing that surprised me: everyone makes fun of officials, bureaucrats, pen pushers, and paper tigers. But that's us! Every one of us who's an employee feels we're an artist, an anarchist, a free spirit, a secret lunatic who recognizes neither norms nor constraints. Every one of us was once promised the kingdom of heaven and none of us wants to acknowledge that we're part of these people we never wanted anything to do with, have been for years, that nothing about us is exceptional, and that it's precisely the sense that we're different that makes us so banal.

"And the children?" Now my voice sounded uncertain. Her saying "you poor thing" to me, just as Luzia said yesterday, hit me with unexpected force.

"Paul insulted his teacher. He's been difficult recently. You need to talk to him on Saturday."

"I can't come home this Saturday. Unfortunately."

"Oh."

"Sunday."

"Fine then, Sunday."

I said something about appointments, things happening unexpectedly, and the appalling chaos in the office. I said something about a new colleague and incompetent workers. Then I had the feeling I was pushing it too far and I stopped talking.

My crew were waiting for me with the usual anxiety. I knew they hated each other and could understand it, that they hated me was in the nature of things, for I too felt a violent aversion for my boss, one Elmar Schmieding from Wattenwil, but why in the world were they afraid of me? I had never made trouble for anybody, and I didn't care what they got up to. I know the system and I know that even medium-serious errors don't cause fundamental upheavals, don't change anything, simply aren't important, they irritate this or that client, but we never hear anything about it and they don't bother us.

So I greeted Schlick and Hauberlan, clapped Smetana on the shoulder, and called a loud "hello" a little emphatically into the room where Lobenmeier and Mollwitz sat opposite each other. Then I sat down at my desk and tried not to think about Luzia. Not about her skin, not about her nose, not about her toes, and absolutely not about her voice. There was a knock, and Mollwitz came in, sweating as usual, struggling under his grotesquely fat body, short, entirely lacking a neck, pathetic.

"Not now!" I said sharply. In a flash he disappeared again. I called Luzia. "Are you free on Saturday?"

"I thought you weren't in the city on weekends."

"How's that?" I got a fright. How did she know that, what had I said to her? "I'm here!"

"Good," she said. "So Saturday."

Another knock, Lobenmeier came in to complain he could no longer put up with Mollwitz.

"Not now!"

He could, said Lobenmeier, put up with a great deal. But at a certain point, enough was enough. That he did absolutely nothing, well okay. That he spent his time posting like a maniac on Internet forums, well okay too. One could even get used to him cursing to himself all the time. But his lack of personal hygiene was more, or perhaps less, than could be tolerated in anyone.

"Lobenmeier," I said gently. "Easy. I'll talk to him and take care of it."

I should have reprimanded him for speaking like that about his colleague, but I couldn't bring myself to do it, the more so since Mollwitz, particularly at the end of the day, really did smell appalling.

On Sunday at around midday I entered my row house in the town by the deep blue lake. Hannah was pale, she had the flu. Paul had shut himself in his room because of some fight, the little one was whining and upset, and I suddenly felt so dizzy it was as if I were drunk. I could still feel Luzia's hands touching me all over my body.

"Till tomorrow?" she'd asked.

"Of course," I'd replied without thinking.

I already knew I'd have to invent something to deceive her, but at the same time the lie seemed insignificant; the only things that did signify were this room and this bed and the woman lying next to me, and my other life, Hannah, the children, this house, were like some implausible fiction—just as now, when I sat down at the table after the long drive, pushed a rubber duck to one side, and looked at Hannah's reddened eyes, Luzia became a distant ghost. I leaned back. The little one stuck her spoon into her mashed potatoes, then smeared the yellow mess all over her face. The phone in my pocket vibrated. A message. Luzia wanted to see me, right away.

"Now what?" asked Hannah. "Not on a Sunday, please."

"They're so incompetent," I said, thumb-clicking: *office emergency, colleague, death.* I pressed Send and had no sense, to my own amazement, that I'd lied—it was as if I really had left another me back there, who was now setting off to the home of the victim: Hauberlan or Mollwitz? Maybe Mollwitz would be better. I nodded in a preoccupied way and left the room to have a serious talk with Paul. After that I'd send Luzia a message describing how I'd arrived in the dead man's apartment and forced myself to be calm and make the first arrangements. Not too many specifics, just the main outlines, plus two or three well-observed details: a door half off its hinges, a cat searching vainly for its little bowl of milk, the label on a bottle of pills. How strange that technology has brought us into a world where there are no fixed places anymore. You speak out of nowhere, you can be anywhere, and because nothing can be checked, anything you choose to imagine is, at bottom, true. If no one can prove to me where I am, if I myself am not absolutely certain, where is the court that can adjudicate these things? Real places anchored in space existed before we had little walkie-talkies and wrote letters that arrived in the same second they were dispatched.

Deep in thought, I switched off the phone in case it suddenly rang. No reception, I'd say, it was always plausible; and God knows network outages were always happening, I knew this, it was my job, my expertise. Then I made a fist, banged on Paul's door, and yelled, "Open Up, Young Man!"

How long can it keep going? I would have said three weeks, maybe a month of danger, freedom, and playing a double game. But the month passed, more weeks went by, and I still wasn't unmasked.

How did it happen in the old days? How did you lie and deceive, how did you have affairs, how did you get away and manipulate and organize your secret activities without the help of ultra-sophisticated technology? I had lived in those times. Yet I could no longer imagine it.

I sent Hannah messages supposedly emanating from Paris and Madrid, Berlin, Chicago, and even, one memorable day, Caracas: I described air yellow with pollution and streets crawling with cars in a hectically charged paragraph which I composed on my laptop in Luzia's kitchen while she stood barefoot and in panties in front of the stove and the autumn rain drummed its fingers against the glass. She dropped a cup of coffee, shards exploded all over the floor, the black liquid formed a Rorschach image.

"What are you writing?"

"An audit report for Longrolf."

And when I told her about poor Longrolf (three children, four wives, alcohol problems, I was now a habitual liar and invented things for no reason at all), I saw myself four days later in my dining room with the little one crawling around on the carpet while Hannah organized holiday photos on the PC which I never used for safety reasons, pictures of the four of us on some overcast beach—having to write Luzia a report on my meeting with the aforesaid Longrolf: the dreariness of the corporate floor, the interoffice intrigues, Longrolf's look of perpetual malice, and Smetana's porcine face, the sheer misery of the whole thing and oh my darling I wish I were back with you. After which I'd slip out to the front of the house ("I'm taking out the garbage!") to prop myself against the wall in the lee of the wind and use my cell phone to call her and tell her how I'd managed to sneak out into the stairwell for a moment just to hear her voice.

A lie? Of course, but hadn't I truly been thinking about her all the time, wasn't I eating my heart out with longing to be near her, while I played with the children or had the same old conversation with Hannah about taxes and the water bill and kindergarten and the mortgage, wasn't I obsessing about her body, her face, and her slightly hoarse voice? What difference did it make whether it was Longrolf who was keeping me away from her or a more or less alienated companion with two noisy children who regarded me as a stranger, and whose existence for as long as I was with them struck me as the product of some confused dream? And conversely, when I locked myself in Luzia's bathroom to run the taps while I talked to Hannah and then the boy ("That noise? It's a bad connection!"), my distant family seemed closer and more dear to me than ever, and Luzia out there in bed a sudden weighty encumbrance like the Congress I'd just claimed to be attending on the phone. I loved them both! And most of all I always loved the one I wasn't with at that moment, the one I couldn't be with, from whom the other one was keeping me separate.

I began to wonder if I was crazy. I woke up in the middle of the night, listened to the breathing of the woman next to me, and wondered for several anxious seconds not so much which one she was, but who I was at this moment and what labyrinth I'd strayed into. Only one step at a time, none of them a large step, none of them difficult, but without realizing it I'd gone so far into it that I could no longer see the way out. I closed my eyes and lay still and surrendered to the cold rush of panic. But when day dawned and I got up and donned each of my roles as if I had no other, everything seemed easy and almost back to normal again.

· · ·

Two days before the Congress of European Telecommunications Providers, I sat in my office on the phone with the babysitter we'd arranged for. Hannah and I wanted to go together, finally we were making time for each other. My presentation was to be short and didn't require any preparation, and the hotel promised luxury and a spa. As I hung up, I saw that an e-mail had just arrived from Luzia. Just one line: *your congress. I'm coming too.*

I rubbed my eyes and thought, as I had every hour of every day, that sooner or later everything was going to explode and a flaming catastrophe was bearing down on me.

"Better not," I wrote, *"a lot of work, dreadful people."*

That's when I realized.

If Luzia knew about the Congress, for I had said nothing about it, that meant she knew someone who was also going to be there. Then I couldn't go with Hannah; far too big a risk that Luzia would hear about it.

And conversely. What if I took Luzia? Hannah didn't know many of my colleagues. She almost never came to this city, and my job had never interested her. But the risk was too great. For a moment I hated both of them.

I called Hannah.

"Oh, what a pity!" She sounded as if her mind were elsewhere, something was preoccupying her completely. I saw her in front of me: buried in a book, eyes bright but dreaming, and the situation—that I wasn't there with her, that I had another woman, that nothing was the way it was supposed to be—brought tears to my eyes.

"It's not going to work," I said. "Have to stay. Too much going on in the office."

"Whatever you think."

"Another time, yes? Soon."

She cleared her throat distractedly. In the background I heard the burble of music on the radio. "Yes, yes, fine."

Luzia's reply popped up on my screen: *ridiculous, it's going to be fun. I need to get out from time to time as well. If you're going, I'm going too. End of discussion!*

"Don't be sad," I said.

"I understand," said Hannah. "I understand."

I hung up. With Luzia it was going to be more difficult, because she was always wanting to know things about my work. Why, when I didn't want to know them myself! But the department had to be represented there: if I went alone, Luzia would come, if I went with Luzia, Hannah would hear about it, if I went with Hannah, Luzia would hear about it; there was only one answer. I summoned Lobenmeier.

Impossible, he said. Trip to Paris. Long planned. Wife's idea. Wedding anniversary.

I called for Schlick.

Impossible! Parents, birthday, big party, only son, had to be there. Besides which, family farm. Outbreak of foot-and-mouth just diagnosed.

I didn't get the connection, but I sighed and let it go, and called Hauberlan, who couldn't because he'd booked a non-refundable cruise to the Hebrides. Smetana was off sick, and my secretary, whom I'd have drafted in desperation, had a long-standing commitment to the National Paintball Championships in a village in Lower Saxony. In no circumstances could she stand in for me. So there was no avoiding it. There was only one last possibility.

Can't do it, I wrote. *Have to send Mollwitz. He has friends in Corporate, he's become too influential.* I had trouble typing, my hands were shaking—with agitation, naturally, but also out of fury with Mollwitz and his intrigues. *So sorry.*

Mollwitz, she replied at once. *Thought he was dead.*

Oh God. Breathe calmly, I thought, calmly. When in doubt, flee forward. *That was another guy with the same name. Strange coincidence.* I looked up. Mollwitz was standing in the door. "You've made it!" I told him authoritatively. "You're leaving tomorrow."

He was sweating more than ever. His little eyes twitched uneasily. He seemed to have put on even more weight recently.

"Don't pretend to be surprised. You're going to represent the department at the Congress. Well played, neatly done, I congratulate you."

Mollwitz panted. Tomorrow, he said quietly, wasn't so good. He had a lot to do. He didn't like traveling. He really did smack his lips when he talked!

"Let's not exaggerate. You know you want to go, I know you want to go, and on the floor above"—I raised my forefinger—"they know too. You'll go far, my friend."

He gave me a pleading look, then decamped. I imagined him next door, back sitting at his desk like a big toad, cursing quietly, and posting online somewhere.

I called Luzia.

It wasn't so bad, she said immediately, it didn't matter, I shouldn't take it to heart.

I nodded silently, already feeling better. She was so good at consoling me.

When Luzia called to tell me she was pregnant, I was at the open-air pool with the children. The sun was playing on the trembling surface of the water, its reflections cut down deep, the whole world seemed shot through with light. Children shrieking, water splashing, the smell of coconut oil, chlorine, and grass.

"What?" I lifted my hand to my brow, but my arm was moving with a delayed action and my fingers seemed to be wrapped in cotton wool. My knees went so weak that I had to sit down. A fat little girl came trotting up, bumped into me, fell over, and began to cry. I blinked. "That's wonderful," I heard myself say.

"Really?" She didn't seem to completely believe me and I didn't quite believe myself either. And yet: why did I feel such a surge of joy? A child—my first! I had never felt so strongly that I was made up of two people, or rather that I had split one and the same life into two different variants. Over there, on the other side of the pool, my daughter was crawling across the grass. Farther in the distance my son was leaning in what was meant to be a casual pose, hoping I couldn't see him and talking to two girls his own age.

"I don't know if I'll be a good father," I said quietly. I stopped, I was finding it hard to speak. "I'll try!"

"You're wonderful! You know, back then when . . . where are you, actually, there's an awful lot of noise!"

"On the street. Not so far from your office. I wish I could come and see you . . ."

"So do it!"

". . . but I can't. An appointment."

"Back then, when I got to know you. I'd never have believed it! You were like someone under a deadweight and at the same time . . . how can I put it? Someone forcing himself to stand upright at all times—I found it hard to believe you." She laughed. "I thought you weren't being honest."

"Strange." My daughter was looking for the edge of the pool. I stood up.

"If anyone had told me back then that it would be you of all people I . . ."

The little one was too near the water. "Can I call you back?" I hurried over toward her.

"But why do you think . . ."

I pressed the disconnect button and began to run. Sharp blades of grass prickled my naked feet. I hurdled two children who were lying there, dodged a dog, pushed a woman aside, and caught my daughter three feet from the water. She looked at me, puzzled, thought for a moment, and began to cry. I lifted her up and whispered soothing nonsense in her ear. *I'll call later,* I thumb-clicked on my phone. *Subway, lousy reception.* I was about to send it, but then added *I'm so happy!* I looked at my daughter's face, and once again was struck by how she was looking more like Hannah with every month that passed. I blew the hair off her forehead, she giggled softly; she'd already forgotten she'd just been crying. I hit Send.

Mollwitz was in a complete state of shock when he got back. He was muttering to himself, was almost un-talkable-to and didn't want to say anything about what had gone on.

Sooner or later, said Hauberlan, it had to happen.

His presentation had been a disaster, said Schlick. Everyone was talking about it. Really embarrassing for the department.

And there was worse, said Lobenmeier. Apparently he'd forced his way into a hotel room and . . .

"Everyone makes mistakes," I said, and they went quiet. It suited them that nothing interested me anymore. I had lost weight and even the classics no longer held my attention, Sallust seemed verbose, Cicero empty, for neither of them addressed the question that preoccupied me to the exclusion of all else, making my mind turn in circles the way water drives a millstone—wasn't it possible to have two houses, two lives, two families, one there, one here, a me in this town and a me in the other one, and two women, each of them as close to me as if she were the only one? It was only a matter of organization, of train timetables and airline schedules, of cleverly judged e-mails and a little foresight in making arrangements. Of course it could all collapse, but it could also ... yes, it could work! For a short while. Or maybe longer.

The double life: the redoubling of life. Only a short time ago I was merely a depressed head of department. How had I come to the point where I suddenly understood them: the bogeymen portrayed in the tabloids, all the people who had secrets just because you can't live without them, and absolute transparency means death, and a single existence is not enough for human beings.

"What?" I jumped. Lobenmeier was standing in front of me. Behind him, Schlick. I hadn't heard them coming. Then I realized that it had happened the other way round. The others had left the room and only these two had stayed behind.

Schlick began to talk in a low voice. Clearly something really terrible had happened: a memo from Security had informed us that several hundred phone numbers in the databank had been given a wrong date for general availability, so there was a danger that although they were already in use, they'd be assigned to new customers. Lobenmeier had forwarded it to Mollwitz, who had set it aside because, as they discovered subsequently, he was absolutely set on writing a post for SpottheStars first.

"For *what*?"

Didn't matter, said Lobenmeier, not important right now. Anyhow, that's what had happened and several dozen new customers had been given already-assigned numbers. The press had got hold of it and at least two claims for commercial damages had already been filed. The main error came from our department.

The screen on my cell phone lit up. Hannah's name, and underneath: *We're coming to visit you!* My pulse began to race.

"We'll talk about this later!" I got to my feet.

He was sorry, said Lobenmeier, but the situation was too serious. It could—

Would, said Schlick.

Lobenmeier nodded. *Would* cost several people their jobs.

I pressed several buttons, but there were no messages. Could I have dreamed it? Had I erased it by mistake? I had to be sure, it was critical that I not make a mistake.

"Be right back," I cried, and ran out down the corridor to the elevator, which took me noisily downstairs, then through the main hall and into the street. That's it, I thought, that's what's happening to me. You don't founder because of circumstances, you don't founder because of bad luck, you founder because of your nerves. You founder because you can't take the pressure. That's how, sooner or later, the truth comes out. I turned around slowly. I noticed that passersby were looking in my direction, that a child on the other side of the street was pointing at me, only to be dragged along by its mother. Pull yourself together, I thought, just pull yourself together, if you don't give up it can work, but you have to pull yourself together. I forced myself to stand there calmly. I glanced at my watch and tried to look like someone mentally checking the day's appointments. Turn around, I told myself, and go back inside. Get in the elevator. They're waiting for you. Sit down behind your desk. Save what can be saved. Do something—defend yourself, don't run away. You're not going to fall apart. Not yet.

"A problem, dear sir?"

Standing next to me was a startlingly thin man with greasy hair, horn-rim glasses, and a bright red cap.

"Excuse me?"

"Life is hard?" he said with an ingratiating smile. It sounded more like a question than a statement. "Every decision is hard, even organizing the everyday things is so complicated that it can drive even the strongest of us mad. You agree, dear sir?"

"What?"

"So many things are not subject to our will, but some things can be made a little easier. I have a taxi at my disposal." He pointed to a black Mercedes standing next to us with the door open. "And here's my suggestion: if there's someone you would like to see in the next hour, call them. Life is over so quickly. That's what these little phones are for, that's why we have all that electrical gadgetry in our pockets. Don't you agree, dear sir?"

I didn't understand what he wanted from me. His appearance was repulsive, but his words had a calming effect on me. "That's a taxi?"

"Dear sir, get in, give me the address, and, you'll see, it'll become one."

I hesitated, but then nodded and let myself sink into the

soft leather of the backseat. He got behind the wheel, took some time adjusting the driver's seat, as if this were not the car he'd come in, repositioned the rearview mirror, and slowly fingered the ignition. "Your address," he said softly. "Please. I know many things but not everything."

I gave it to him.

"We'll be there in a flash." He turned on the engine and steered out into the traffic. "Are you sure you want to go home? Not somewhere else? No one you'd like to visit?"

I shook my head, pulled out my phone, and dialed Luzia's number. "Come to me!"

"Now?"

"Now."

"What are you doing here anyway? I thought you had to be in Zurich for the whole week! Did something happen?"

I rubbed my forehead. Right, I had said that, so that I could get away the next day and spend the weekend with Hannah. "It didn't come off."

"Mollwitz again?"

"Mollwitz again."

"I'm on my way."

I disconnected and stared at the phone's tiny screen. And if Hannah really was on her way here? Then I'd done the exact wrong thing, and Luzia couldn't come anywhere near my apartment. I'd have to call right away—but which one of them? Why were things slipping away from me already? The thin man stared at me in the rearview mirror. I felt faint, and closed my eyes.

"You're asking yourself why so many things aren't doable, dear sir? Because a man wishes to be many things. In the literal sense of the word. He wishes to be multiple. Diverse. He'd like to have several lives. But only superficially, not deep down. The ultimate aspiration, dear friend, is to become one. One with oneself, one with the universe."

I opened my eyes. "What are you talking about?"

"I didn't say a word. And if I had, it wouldn't be anything you don't already know."

"Is this even your car?"

"Should that really be your most pressing concern?"

I fell silent until he halted outside my apartment building. For some reason I'd assumed he wouldn't take any money, but he named a wildly high fare. I paid and got out; when I looked back, the car was already gone.

Luzia was waiting in the corridor outside the door of my apartment. She must have set off immediately. You could really rely on her. "What is it?" she asked. "What?" She was looking at me attentively.

I opened my mouth and shut it again.

She put her hands on my shoulders. "Is there something you want to tell me?"

I didn't move. We were still standing in the corridor. I took a deep breath and didn't say a thing.

We went inside. Through the hallway, through my untidy living room, and then, as always, into the bedroom.

Seconds later we were lying there and I felt the firmness of her limbs, saw close up the darkness of her eyes. Her hands fumbled with my belt, my hands slid under her blouse, all of their own accord, without hesitation or reflection, it seemed to happen without our intervention. Then the covers and the nakedness and the panting and her strong hands, her clutching me and me clutching her and then we were already apart again, lying exhausted beside each other, out of breath. There was a thin coating of sweat on her skin. The sight made me melt, to such a degree that I was on the point of saying things that I would have needed to take back a few minutes later. Was she really carrying my child? But I already had two, and they were difficult and disconcerting enough, they looked at me suspiciously and asked questions to which I had no answers, and I wasn't a good father to them.

"It can't go on like this," she said.

My stomach went into spasm. "What?"

"This Mollwitz. You're too nice. You have to do something."

I slid my hand under her neck. How soft her hair was. The golden fuzz on her arms. The soft curve of her breast. I would have done anything for her and abandoned anything.

Anything?

Anything except the other one who would call me in a few minutes or perhaps next week or next month or sometime this year at the most inconvenient moment, to tell me that she was coming for a surprise visit and was already in town, on my street or already in the building, on the stairs, right in front of my door. If this were a story, I thought, there would be no point in delaying things, and it would happen right now.

The doorbell rang. I sat up with a jerk.

"What is it?" asked Luzia.

"The bell."

"I didn't hear anything."

I stroked her head in silence. I can still confess everything, I thought, I haven't yet been convicted of anything. Would you forgive me? But I knew she wouldn't.

Without pulling on my clothes, I went out into the hallway. If I opened the door now and Hannah was standing outside, what should I do? Maybe there was a way to fake my way out of it. In films and stage farces there's always one, just as everything looks hopeless. The leading actors find the most brilliant subterfuges, open and slam doors, push one woman into one room and the other into another, they maneuver whole groups of people around the smallest spaces without anyone bumping into anyone else. An entire genre specialized in nothing else. Anyone with sufficient determination could surely do the same thing. Almost anything could be accomplished with the necessary strength of mind. Even a double life. But who has it, I asked myself as I stood there naked in the hallway; who has that kind of strength?

I reached for the handle. Even the certainty that there's absolutely nothing now between you and catastrophe gives a certain assurance. For one last moment I hesitated. Why not have an even bigger scene, an even more powerful effect? If Hannah was standing outside, why not the children too, why not my parents as well, come of their own accord from their dismal retirement home, and while we were at it, why not Lobenmeier, Hauberlan, and Longrolf from Accounting, why not Mollwitz too; all come to see me without my clothes on, without secrets, pretences, illusions, and deceptions, just as I really was.

"Come in." I opened the door. "Come in, everyone!"

In Danger

I thought we were going to crash. My God, have you ever been through anything like that?"

Elisabeth shook her head. This time she too had thought this was it: the tiny plane had emitted cracks and groans as it was carried by huge gusts of wind and the packages of medicines had been hurled around in every direction in the cargo bay that stank of metal and gasoline. One of the doctors had been struck in the head, and they'd had to put a pressure bandage on it to stanch the flow of blood. But Leo had sat there calmly the whole time, pale but upright, a narrow, crooked smile on his face.

"I wonder," he tilted his head back, stretched his arms, and turned around, "why we find this beautiful. Some grass, a few trees, a lot of sky. Why is it like coming home?"

"Not so loud!" She felt dizzy, she had to sit down on the ground for a moment: no asphalt, just reddish earth, flattened hard by the wheels of planes. At the edges of the runway two jeeps were waiting with a number of men in uniform. Two of them were carrying machine guns slung across their bodies.

"A dream from the distant past," said Leo. "Millions of years on the savannah. Everything subsequent a mere episode. Tell me, are you feeling sick?"

"It's okay," she murmured: there was a dull coughing sound and the plane started the propellers: rotating at first, then a gray blur. The machine began to taxi. Müller and Rebenthal, the two doctors, loaded the cartons of medicines onto the jeeps. From time to time one of them cast skeptical glances at Leo. Nobody had been pleased that Elisabeth had come with a companion this time. It wasn't customary, it wasn't done; and if anyone were to find out that the nervous guest was in fact a writer whose job it was to spill everything he saw, she would never be forgiven. But Leo had insisted; he wanted, he kept on saying, to learn her world too, and real life couldn't go on escaping him. So, perhaps because she wanted finally to show him this real life, perhaps because she was curious how he would handle himself under real pressure, but perhaps also because she just couldn't refuse his wishes, she had finally taken him along.

"Is that a real weapon?" he asked the two doctors. "The one the man over there's carrying, there, you see, the one in the jeep, is it real?"

"What do you think?" asked Müller. He was a tall, taciturn Swiss who'd worked for years in the Congo and had gone through things there he never talked about. When he'd been hit in the head by the crate during the flight, he hadn't even groaned.

"Let me help!" Leo snatched the carton out of his hands and set it in the back of the jeep. There was a clink of glass. "Have you read Hemingway? I think about him all the time here. Can you work here *without* thinking of him?"

"Yes," said Müller. "Easily."

"But all this," Leo pointed to the armed men, then the plane, which was just turning at the end of the runway, "could be straight out of one of his books!"

"Don't point, please!" said Rebenthal.

"What?"

"Don't point with your finger."

"It could make them angry," said Müller. "That's certainly not what you want."

"But these are your people!"

"Leo," said Elisabeth. "Please."

"But—"

"Be quiet and go sit in the jeep!"

How could she explain to him? How to make clear to an outsider what compromises had to be made when working in a war zone, how to say to him that you settled for the less murderous faction or the one you thought was less murderous, or you just paid one of them, no matter which, for shelter and protection. She had lived in murderers' camps more than once, had eaten their bread and their soup, and then treated those people in destroyed villages whom her hosts had left alive. Nothing was clean, no decision was clear, you could only try to help the wounded and ask no questions.

"Look!" cried Leo.

She followed his glance. At the end of the runway the plane left the ground, climbed, grew small, and disappeared into the blazing corona of the sun.

"To crash here," he said. "That would be something. Would sound good in someone's biography. Lost in Africa."

Elisabeth shrugged.

"Since Maria Rubinstein went missing a year ago her books have never been more popular. Now they want to give her the Romner Prize even *in absentia*. My God, can you imagine, I could have taken that trip. Then maybe it would be me and not her—I still keep asking myself if I should feel guilty."

Elisabeth bobbed her head. She had no idea what he was talking about.

Then they were sitting squashed together in the jeep, driving through the tall grass. The wind blew through their hair, it smelled of earth, the sun above them was enormous; it was so bright they had to squeeze their eyes shut and everything dissolved in the light. Leo called something, she couldn't understand a word. In the distance she heard the dark rumble of thunder.

"What did you say?" she cried.

"Real for the first time," yelled Leo.

"What?"

"I can't remember when something was as real as this."

She didn't want to know what he meant, there were other things she had to think about. Tomorrow she would start dealing with the first wounded, and she knew that once this started she would be cut off from all feeling. Everything would become soft and cottony, and while she was doing what needed to be done, there would only be a dull numbness inside her. How often already had she decided to stay in Europe and not do this work anymore? Next to her, Leo was pulling out his notebook and beginning to scribble. What was he thinking, did he take himself for André Malraux? She peered over his shoulder but could only make out a few words: *Living room . . . switch off the TV . . . playground . . . neighbor.*

He turned and saw her look. "Just an idea!" he cried. "That's all."

The dappled head of a hyena rose for a moment in the grass. The soldier behind them aimed his weapon but didn't shoot and in a moment they had passed it. Leo kept making notes and she couldn't help staring at the notebook. Her old fear that he would put her in a story and create a distorted copy of her, rearranged according to his own needs: the thought was unbearable. But whenever she said this, he evaded her or changed the subject.

Back there in the capital, he had been strangely calm. During her conversations with two ministers he had stood by her side without drawing any attention to himself, but not missing a word. After two days during which there was no water, he had made no protests but like all of them had washed first using mineral water and then had not washed at all, and on their last day he'd secretly paid their driver to take him through the slum where the worst atrocities had taken place. She only heard about it afterward. Apparently Leo had even gotten out of the car and asked people questions. Where did his sudden courage come from? It wasn't like him. The thunder echoed in the distance again. Instinctively she looked up at the sky, but there was nothing but a few scattered high clouds.

"I've never heard shots," said Leo. "Artillery?"

"Tanks," said Müller.

Of course! She closed her eyes for a moment. Was it possible he'd recognized the sound and she hadn't?

The village was a mere grouping of little corrugated iron huts. Two rusty jeeps were standing at an angle in the grass, a dozen men, weapons at the ready, sat yawning around the remains of a fire. A goat was sniffing thoughtfully at a mound of earth. Three Europeans ducked out of one of the houses: a little woman in her mid-fifties with glasses and a knitted vest, a man in uniform with the UN insignia on the front, and behind them a woman with brown hair, tall, slim, and extremely beautiful.

"Riedergott," said the little woman. Elisabeth took a moment to realize she'd just introduced herself. "Klara Riedergott, Red Cross. Good that you're here."

"Rotmann," said the man. "UNPROFOR. The situation is completely unstable. I don't know how long we can maintain a presence here."

A phone rang, they all looked around, puzzled. Finally Leo pulled out his gadget with an apologetic smile. How amazing that there was reception here! He turned away and began to murmur.

"Haven't we already met?" asked Elisabeth.

"I can't think where," said Mrs. Riedergott.

"Yes," said Elisabeth. "Not so long . . ."

"I already told you," Mrs. Riedergott had turned rigid. "I can't think where!"

Elisabeth noticed that the brown-haired woman was looking at her. She had an aura of intelligence and something secret. For some reason she seemed to be the most important person here. It was almost impossible not to look at her.

"The Elmitz Karner Prize," cried Leo.

"Excuse me?"

"I'm getting the Elmitz Karner Prize. They wanted to know if I'd accept. I said I can't possibly think about such nonsense right now."

"And?"

"What do I know? Probably they'll give it to someone else. Can't pay attention to that sort of thing right now. They must be confusing me with someone who does give a damn."

Elisabeth's eyes moved back to the woman. What in the world was going on here? Her suspicions were still vague, she couldn't put them into words. At that moment the horizon glittered, despite the brightness of the daylight, and she thought the ground trembled. Only seconds later did they hear the explosion. I shouldn't have brought him here, she thought, it's too much for him. But Leo looked calm and alert, only his lips twitched a little.

"I don't think they're coming in this direction," he said. "They're heading north. They'll probably stick to their route."

"Looks that way," said Rotmann.

"You never know," said Rebenthal.

"How," she said, "do you know which way is north?"

"Are there elephants here?" asked Leo.

"They're all on the other side of the border," said Rotmann. "Fleeing the war."

"I came to Africa," said Leo. "Perhaps I'll die in Africa. Without seeing an elephant." He smiled in the direction of the brown-haired woman. She returned his look. There was a complicity in it that went far beyond words, a total mutual understanding, of the kind that only exists between people who know each other to the very core.

Elisabeth felt her pulse beat faster. "Someone needs to inventory the stocks of medicines," Rotmann said to her. "Would you help me?" And it was true, this was not the moment to be thinking about such things, there was work to be done.

The two of them sat down inside one of the stifling huts and sorted injection ampoules. Rotmann squeezed his eyes to slits in order to see better. He was breathing heavily. Beads of sweat stood out on his moustache.

"Why UNPROFOR?" Elisabeth asked suddenly.

"Pardon?"

"UNPROFOR was in Yugoslavia, UN Peacekeeping Forces should be called something different here."

He said nothing for a few minutes. "I must have misspoken." He laughed awkwardly. "I do know who I work for."

"And who do you work for?"

He looked at her, baffled. Outside there was the sound of further artillery fire. The door opened, the brown-haired woman came in and bent over the medicines.

"Excuse me." A handshake, both soft and strong. "A pleasure to meet you. I'm Lara Gaspard."

"You're . . ." Elisabeth rubbed her forehead. "Weren't you . . . in America?"

"A long story. Very complicated. My whole life is one long story of complications."

"Astonishing," said Rotmann, "how alike you two look."

"You think?" asked Lara.

Elisabeth stood up and went out without saying a word.

She leaned against the metal hut wall. It was still hot, but the light was fading from minute to minute. In a moment it would be dark, near the equator this happened very fast. It took her several seconds to realize that Leo was standing next to her.

"All this isn't real," she said. "Or is it?"

"Depends on your definition." He lit a cigarette. "Real. It's a word that means so much, it doesn't mean anything anymore."

"That's why you're so serene. So composed and on top of everything. This is your version, this is what you've made of it. Out of our trip back then and out of what you know of my work. And of course Lara is there."

"Lara is always there when I am."

"I knew you'd do this. I knew I'd end up in one of your stories! Exactly what I didn't want!"

"We're always in stories." He drew on the cigarette, the tip glowed red, then he lowered it and blew smoke into the warm air. "Stories within stories within stories. You never know where one ends and another begins! In truth, they all flow into one another. It's only in books that they're clearly divided."

"The mistake with UNPROFOR shouldn't have happened. Ever heard of research?"

"I'm not that kind of author."

"Could be," she said. "And I'm going to leave you."

He looked at her. She felt a wave of sadness well up in her. The horizon glittered again. Out there was death, out there reality was so harsh and so painful that there were no words to describe it. No matter whether he'd thought it up or she was actually here—there were places of pure terror, and places where things were themselves and nothing else.

"But not now," he said. "Not in this story."

They were silent for some moments. In front of them the uniformed men had lit the fire. Now they were sitting around the flames talking quietly in their language. From time to time, one of them laughed.

"In reality you'd never turn down a prize. Give me a cigarette."

"That was my last."

"Nothing to be done?"

He shook his head. "My God, no. And yet I badly need more, I'm appallingly nervous."

She blinked, but she could hardly see him anymore. He struck her as unreal, already almost transparent and more of a placeholder than himself. And inside the hut meantime, she knew, Lara Gaspard's presence and charisma had only grown stronger.

"Poor Mrs. Riedergott! Did you really have to use her too?"

"Why not?" His voice was almost disembodied, it seemed to be coming from all around and yet was almost inaudible in the evening wind. "I found her very useful."

"Useful."

"Is that bad?"

She shrugged and went back inside. Lara Gaspard was holding a pencil and drawing in a sketchbook with dream-like concentration. How graceful she was! Beside her Rotmann was reading a worn French paperback, *The Art of Being Oneself* by Miguel Auristos Blanco. Müller and Rebenthal were playing cards with one of the militiamen.

"Sometimes he deals," Müller whispered. "Sometimes we deal, then we look at the cards and he tells us who's won. What the hell kind of game is that?"

Elisabeth shrugged to show she had no idea what kind of game it was. She sat down and leaned her head against the wall. She was dead tired, but she wanted to stay awake. What kind of dreams would she find herself in if she fell asleep? "So where's Leo?"

Müller looked up. "Who?"

Elisabeth nodded. That's how they did it, that's how they evaded their responsibilities. Already he was everywhere, behind things, and above the sky and beneath the earth like a second-class God, and there was no remaining possibility to hold him accountable.

"We should go to sleep." Lara Gaspard closed the sketch-book. "Tomorrow will be a hard day."

Elisabeth shut her eyes. Mind you, if this was a story, something would happen and things would become hard, and if they didn't become hard, then it wasn't a story. Where was sleep going to take her? Suddenly she didn't care. Her phone rang. She paid no attention.

Daniel Kehlmann was born in 1975 in Munich, the son of a director and an actress. He attended a Jesuit school in Vienna, traveled widely, and has won several awards for previous novels and short stories, among them the 2005 Candide Award, the 2006 Kleist Award, and the 2008 Thomas Mann Award. His works have been translated into more than forty languages, and his novel *Measuring the World* became an instant best seller in several European countries, selling more than 1.5 million copies. Kehlmann lives in Vienna and Berlin.

A NOTE ON THE TYPE

This book was set in Granjon, a type named in compli-
ment to Robert Granjon, a type cutter and printer active
in Antwerp, Lyons, Rome, and Paris from 1523 to 1590.
Granjon, the boldest and most original designer of his
time, was one of the first to practice the trade of type-
founder apart from that of printer. Granjon more closely
resembles Garamond's own type than do any of the various modern faces that bear his name.

Composed by Creative Graphics,
Allentown, Pennsylvania
Printed and bound by RR Donnelley,
Harrisonburg, Virginia
Designed by Wesley Gott